Starwood Dreams

THE NORTH STAR B&B SERIES

MOLLY SUMMERS

Want A FREE Clean Romance Book?

Tap here to get your FREE book!

CHAPTER 1
A Dream

C *lack.*

"Meeting adjourned." Those long-awaited words were a relief after a drawn out divorce with many pauses and renegotiations. It shouldn't have come as a surprise to Sylvie that something could sound so simple and turn so complicated, everything else in her marriage felt like an assembly line of impossibilities. Why should their divorce proceedings be any different?

But none of that mattered now because she was stepping out into the smoggy air of lower Manhattan, walking down the steps of the courthouse with her sister and best friend on either side of her. Though the cruel string of wounds rehashed crippled the troughs of her broken heart, there was something stirring inside of her.

A light that she had thought burnt out, a spark she had forgotten she was capable of having, it made her trepidatious almost as much as it lured her. A call, simple and prominent, whispered between honking horns, sirens, and bumbling traffic...

Remember your dream, it whispered, and she stopped in her tracks. Meera and Lyla walked on ahead until they noticed she'd stopped moving. It's strange how the happiest memories can become sources of pain, sadness. Especially when they haven't been part of your reality for such a long time.

2 Years Ago

Sylvie's hand touched a papery smooth surface on top of her hardwood dresser just as the sun peeked through the blinds of her empty master suite, her eyes flew open in shock. Surely he had not left her a note, like he used to. But maybe...

A small chirping bird of hope spread its wings, as she turned over to watch it plummet to the ground before ever taking flight. Dread split her right down the center as she squinted at the papers covering her phone, which was beginning to buzz. Everything left in her, shattered in that moment. There in her hand was not a love letter like the ones her husband used to leave for her scattered about the house. Instead, it was divorce papers with a green stick-it note stuck to the top that read:

"I can't do this anymore."

She wanted to crumple it up or tear it like he had her heart by hammering this last nail in the proverbial coffin of their dead marriage. Instead, her hands only shook as she read his note to her over and over again.

I can't do this anymore. I can't do this anymore. I can't do this anymore. I can't do this anymore...

The backs of her eyes ached, and her phone was still ringing as if it hadn't realized how insignificant it was at that moment. Her world was spinning so fast it was on the brink of spontaneous combustion.

She forced a hand to reach for the phone, throat tight and eyes stinging with fresh tears that barely permitted her to answer, "Yes?"

"Oh my God, Sylvie..." She could tell by her sister Lyla's tone that she was about to go on some rant about one of the mothers on the volunteer committee at church. Or some other trivial thing that seemed so small in comparison to this devastation, but Sylvie still let her go on.

"I've been trying to get ahold of you all morning, where have you been? Are you sleeping the entire day again? I can come make you dinner tonight, if you need me to."

Sylvie thought about it for a moment, fingers tracing the bumps of ink on the pages in her hands. "Okay. Yes."

"Yes?"

"Yes, please come over." She forced out a feeble attempt to sound somewhat normal.

"Okay. I'll be over in twenty."

Then, the line went silent, and Sylvie placed her phone on the bedside table. It was so quiet in the house she could hear the traffic outside her New York City townhouse. Those sounds felt like home, almost as much as the sounds of her children carrying on in the background. But they weren't children any more and every room in her home was vacant, even her own most days. She stood, crossing to the window and looking out at the city as the sun found its usual place in the sky.

"Good morning," she whispered to herself when she really wanted to crawl back in bed and have a good cry. She had an excuse to do it. Every excuse, actually. Though she'd decided to try to hold it together, at least until her sister left after dinner. She didn't want to explain any of this to anyone, not yet at least. Speaking about it would only make it far too real.

The doorbell rang exactly twenty minutes later. Sylvie had managed to get dressed in that amount of time—throwing on a light sweater, some loose jeans, and even pulling her hair up into a top-knot. It was the most put-together she had been in a year. After another second of fiddling with the pieces of hair falling in her face, the doorbell rang a few more times.

"Coming!" She yelled loud enough for Lyla to hear. At least, she thought it was loud enough. Apparently, it hadn't been, because the bell rang all the way up until she galloped down the stairs and pulled the door open. Lyla stood, paper bags full of groceries stuffed under each arm and eyes bouncing up and down Sylvie's fresh clothes.

"You look..." She shook her head stepping inside as she closed the door behind her. "Are you feeling alright? You haven't worn proper clothes in at least a year, maybe more. Not to say you ever look bad, but right now, you look better than ever." Lyla's quick words were intentionally careful as she turned toward the hallway that led to the kitchen.

"Thanks." Sylvie pulled at her sweater, following her sister into the kitchen and trying to look normal, whatever normal was for her now. Lyla sat the groceries down in a huff before turning back to her, eyes filled with a cautious sympathy. Sylvie despised the look because it only made her want to tell her everything right then and there.

"I can message Meera, too." Her brows lowered as she turned towards the shelf containing brass pots and pans.

"You don't need to do that." Sylvie shook her head, feeling guilty that everyone always came to her aid when she was in need. That wasn't the way things were supposed to end up. Sylvie was always the one that cared for others, and loved seeing them happy, safe, fulfilled even. She must have really been broken beyond repair if this was her new normal. The thought made her even more determined not to crack under the weight of their kindness.

Lyla launched into a conversation of her own as she often did, already laying out the list of events for the rest of the day while the sound of clinking glasses, clanking plates, and constant chatter resounded throughout the kitchen. Lyla was in another world. A world Sylvie wasn't cognizant enough to participate in as her mind trailed to other places.

So, she only nodded along as Lyla zipped around her in a flurry. Life felt surreal, distant, and intangible. She knew she was alive still, but her brain was distant from her body. The daylight passed through the windows just as quickly as Lyla worked, and before long, every spotlight shone in the kitchen, illuminating the savory steam floating from the pots on the stove.

Somehow the day had passed, and she was sitting with a glass of wine that she'd barely touched, listening to the music Lyla had turned on while she was cooking.

The doorbell rang just as Lyla pulled fresh bread out of the oven. The sound of the familiar chimes pulled Sylvie back to reality, and the fuzziness of her mind was all that remained as an after effect of disconnecting from everything during the hours that had passed.

"That's Meera!" Lyla looked toward Sylvie as she stirred one of the pots on the stove with a new fury. "Grab it?"

Sylvie nodded, not remembering when Lyla had the time to invite Meera. Especially since she had told her it wasn't necessary. Meera could squeeze anything out of Sylvie, even when she didn't mean to. Acting normal would be even more crucial with her present. Sliding off the bar stool she had been sitting on, legs stiff, she made her way to the front door. Even though the sky had been darkened by clouds most of the day, the night felt especially so as she grabbed the door handle. Sylvie opened the door to see her best friend standing with arms wide open. It was as if every dark cloud had been blown away by the sunshine Meera always seemed to bring wherever she went.

"Hi, Sylvie." She wrapped Sylvie up in the warmth of her embrace, comfort radiating from her as she stepped inside.

"Just in time for dinner!" Lyla shouted from the kitchen, excited that her plan had been going accordingly.

Meera rolled her eyes as she pulled away, causing Sylvie to let out a laugh. A real one, nothing forced. Nothing was ever forced when it came to Meera. It was only because they had known each other for most of their lives, and as a result could tell what the other was thinking so much of the time.

"So glad you invited me *so* ahead of schedule, Lala. It's not like I live in the Bronx or anything." Meera rolled her beautiful big brown eyes again with a sarcastic huff.

"What's that?" Lyla popped her head around the corner, but Meera shook her head, wrapping an arm around Sylvie.

"Just happy to be here, that's all."

Lyla narrowed her eyes at Meera before slowly retreating back into the kitchen, and the two of them giggled together.

"How are you really?" Meera whispered to Sylvie, studying her face with purpose and a concern so deep it pulled her thick brows together.

Sylvie attempted to nod, but it turned into more of a shake, and Meera pulled her back into a tight hug.

"I have an idea," she whispered before linking arms with Sylvie and bringing her into the kitchen. "I have an idea," she repeated louder for all of them to hear.

Lyla turned around, eyebrows arched in an unenthusiastic anticipation.

"We should take a trip to the beach. Sylvie, you know

8

you've always loved the beach... You know how you used to have that dream?"

She still had that dream, but she only nodded for Meera to continue.

"Well, I was thinking that we could go on a trip. Just the husbands and wives. Obviously, my Sahil will be with us in spirit, looking down on us as we sip cocktails by the water... But it could be so much fun!" Her eyes darted between Sylvie and Lyla, who looked to be considering it more than Sylvie.

"That could be really good for you, actually." Lyla finally pointed to Sylvie whose eyes accidentally grew round.

"What do you think?" Meera squeezed her arm excitedly.

"It could be a marriage reset for you and Jameson..." Lyla said, like a dagger to her wounded heart.

"And you both could have alone time... I'll bring my books with me, and Lyla will have Albert."

"Yes, and we could go fishing or something rustic like that." Lyla clapped excitedly, and Meera added on. Before long, they were staying in some random cabin that may or may not exist, doing group activities, like some hallmark movie where things incvitably always go wrong. Except they had gone wrong already, and the trip would never take place because...

"I'm getting a divorce." She barely spit out the words in such a pathetic haggled way that it made Lyla go instantly silent—a rarity. Meera's sharp inhale of shock made the first tear roll down Sylvie's cheek as the two of them looked between one another.

"What happened?" Lyla finally asked, a little bit of judgment in her tone that made Sylvie want to leave the room and give her no explanation. But she wanted to do everything in her power to avoid being alone.

"He ended it."

"That good-for-nothing—" She stopped herself, taking a breath before continuing. "He's not even worth my insults." She lifted her nose as Meera wrapped an arm around Sylvie."Trash. He's trash, Sylvie. You don't deserve this."

Sylvie tried to believe her friend's words, but she just couldn't. It wasn't that she didn't trust them, it was that she no longer trusted herself. Everything she had done was what had caused this final stage of her decaying marriage.

How could she live with herself knowing she had played such a starring role in the breaking of her family, or tell their children the news, or live in a home so stuffed with their memories?

She looked past them at the picture above her fireplace. A picture of the family vacation to Hawaii hung proudly. She could practically hear Theo's muffled giggles, her eldest's mouth full of sand on a dare from her youngest, Ezra. Her two girls, June and Eleanor, grimaced in disgust, their eyes looking over at the boys with horror.

All she had wanted was a nice family photo, one for their wall, but every time she tried to get the perfect shot, one of the kids would do something crazy. Her husband had just chuckled when she complained about it, scooping her up into his arms.

"Memories are made whether everything looks perfect or not, Sylvia May," he'd say, calming her irritation only slightly. He was wrong about countless things, but she could admit he was right about that. Those silly pictures ended up being some of her favorites when they got home, and even more so, after everything began to fracture and fray with what-if's.

One thing was certain, her life was about to change, but whether that would be good, was uncertain —*everything* was uncertain.

Present Day

"Sylvie... You've got this look in your eye..." Lyla stepped cautiously toward her.

"I see it, too." Meera nodded as they made slow strides closer.

Sylvie didn't care, though, she had made up her mind the moment she realized what she wanted. What she always wanted.

"Come on, let's get you home." Lyla reached for the sleeve of her pale blue petticoat, and Sylvie yanked her arm away. Lyla's eyes grew round, lips parted as she looked at Meera. In their eyes, Sylvie was a ticking time bomb. She knew that, she knew that was why they were reacting with such cautiousness. But Sylvie shook her head all the same.

"I'm not going home." She looked between them both with a slight grin, genuine and determined.

"What do you mean—"

"I'm going to Massachusetts," she blurted over the top of Lyla's hesitant question.

"You're what?" Meera asked, usually the one on board with whimsical spurs such as this. Sylvie wouldn't let their immediate confusion get the best of her, though. She straightened her back, standing her ground.

"My dream." She cocked her brows up implicitly in Meera's direction, and Meera's face creased as she searched something in the air. Then, recognition leaked across her face as she lifted her chin knowingly.

"Sylvie, I don't know...don't you think..."

As Meera searched for the words, Lyla jumped in. "What are we talking about?"

Her eyes flicked between the two of them.

"It's just this bed and breakfast idea she had when we were little." She waved a hand as if dismissing it as a childish fantasy. "I thought you decided it wasn't for you?"

"No, Jameson decided it wasn't for me... I've always wanted it. You know how much I love to care for people and how deeply I love small beach-town living."

Lyla was clearly still stuck on the idea being preposterous because her head was shaking like a bobble head. "A bed and breakfast? After this massive, drawn out divorce, you want to get into another lengthy and arduous process? Sis, this seems too hasty. Maybe if you take some time to think about it more—"

"I've thought about it my whole life. I'm sure it's what I want. I'm done wasting time doing things that everyone else thinks I should. My kids are grown, I'm alone, and I have a settlement that can at least get me up and running." Sylvie was already walking away, headed right for the road to wave down a cab instead of taking the car that her sister drove them all in.

"Where are you going?" Lyla called after her, but a cab was already pulling over to let her in. It had been years since she'd done this, and a part of her was beginning to feel like a version of herself she had long forgotten. This small taste of excitement made her smile uncontrollably, just as Meera came up behind her.

Her warm breath puffed clouds in the early spring cold as she grabbed Sylvie's arm and hauled her toward their car.

"What are you doing?" She fought back, twisting her body and attempting to find some way to dig her boots into the crumby gray sidewalk.

"If you're going to insist on this, we're coming with you." She grunted, stopping right at the open car door that Lyla was holding. Sylvie stopped, tilting her head at Meera in question. Did she really mean it? Or was this a ruse to get her back home?

Meera's sincerity nodded back, her dark hair dropping over her shoulder.

"But what about work?" she asked Meera. "And what about the kids and Albert?"

"We'll figure it out," Meera gently proclaimed.

"Together," Lyla confirmed. And there was no hesitancy between the two of them. They seemed genuine, probably concerned about her, but nonetheless transparent. She could believe them, all that was left was to keep believing in herself, and maybe that would be enough to make her lofty dream a lasting reality.

"So, where are we going?" Lyla asked as everyone buckled their seatbelts, and Sylvie flicked through the list on her phone of ideal towns. She went to the one at the top of the list, a town at the very tip of Massachusetts, right past Nantucket. A town so small it could be walked across in less than an hour, rested right at the crescent of its very own beach.

With eyes aglow like a child's on Christmas morning, she called to the front of the car, "Starwood. Starwood, Massachusetts."

CHAPTER 2

The Accident

"There it is!" Sylvie practically squealed, pressing her finger to the window as they passed the sign welcoming them into Starwood. Meera's apprehensive eyes titled to Lyla's, but Sylvie didn't care. If they couldn't see it right then, they would in time. This was everything she ever wanted, and if anything, the divorce had caused her to realize it even more so.

"Is it 226, or 266?" Lyla asked, glancing into the back seat through the mirror. Sylvie glanced down at her phone. The image of the rental property shone on the screen. She smiled without intending to as she scrolled through the details from the property owncr who had approved their stay just after an hour of her applying.

"226!" She clarified just as Lyla took an abrupt turn down a quaint little neighborhood. The tall wispy grass swayed on either side of them, and white sand lined the edge of the road. The sun shone through the tall trees, creating leaf patterns on the ground and the windows of their car passing by.

"The houses are cute." Meera's voice sounded forced as she craned her neck to Sylvie.

"I think so, too. I love the light blues and cream wood paneling."

"It's certainly beachy." Lyla added as the turn signal clicked to the right, the final turn into their driveway. It was long, a dirt path with sprawling fields on either side, all the way up to a Cape Cod looking home with beautiful stone accents and a deep blue wood that appeared to be freshly painted.

As Lyla put the car in park, Sylvie looked on the house in awe. It was the first tangible step to seeing her dreams come to life. Though it was only their temporary living quarters, this town would be permanent. And she liked the sense of accomplishment just that realization was already giving her.

The hollow clack of the door opening reconnected her to the task at hand and to Meera's grin, helping her out of the car. She took it and slid down until her sneakers collided with the sandy driveway.

"This is it, Meera. I can feel it." She whispered to her as she grabbed her arm gleefully. Lyla closed the trunk with a huff before joining Sylvie's other side. She wrapped an arm around her sister and best friend, looking on at the home one more time before intending to enter it.

"So, I love this *spontaneity*. I do..." Lyla lied. Sylvie knew she never ever enjoyed spontaneity. I just wasn't in her nature.

"But…" Meera lowered her chin to her.

"How long are we meant to be here?"

"I told you when we packed your things that I'm staying here for good." Sylvie felt her brows crease her forehead as she studied Lyla's concern.

"Right, but…I only packed for a few weeks."

Meera chuckled flippantly. "It's a good thing this town has clothing stores." This comment earned her a glare from Lyla, just before Sylvie broke away from them and headed up the driveway to the front porch steps.

The house was even more majestic, the closer she got. The front door, a creamy white with glass paneling carved out like rays of sun. She followed the owner's instructions for getting inside by lifting the bristly welcome mat and grabbing the two gold house keys.

They seemed to shine in between her fingers, like an unwavering hope as she stuck the key in the hole and turned until the lock clicked. Her other hand shook with anticipation as she turned the handle and pushed the door open. The house felt cool and breezy, a lot like the outside, but slightly less damp. It was like jumping into a pool on a hot summer day when she stepped inside.

There were no pictures of her family or memories to haunt her here. She could keep the ones she wanted in her heart without being constantly reminded of the ones that hurt too much. She breathed in the fresh scent of cotton and lemons, and her heart fluttered at the reality before her.

The entire home was so bright and airy. Dark wood floors, large open windows, white walls evenly decorated with beach-themed decor—seashells, wood plaques, and sea glass—and the comfiest looking furniture. It was the perfect mixture of home and vacation. She hoped to emulate these feelings in her bed and breakfast. Her friends stepped inside, suitcases in hand, looking more worn out than she felt.

"We're going to go find our rooms and take a nap," Lyla said, large dark glasses still resting on the tip of her small nose as she brushed past Sylvie and right up the creaky wood steps.

"You should try to get some rest, too. We had a long day." Meera nudged Sylvie's shoulder softly and followed Lyla up the steps.

"What about dinner?"

"I'm too tired for food."

Sylvie checked the silver watch on her wrist. "It's only seven..."

Meera paused, turning around to look down at her.

"We've got a long week ahead of us if you're going to meet with realtors about the bed and breakfast. I think if you sleep now, it will be easier to get everything done tomorrow. I know you're excited about everything, but please, just try to get some rest. It might even help you think more clearly."

Why did she need to think more clearly? Was Meera more on Lyla's side than she had thought? She was capable of making her own decisions, and she certainly didn't need anyone along for the ride who didn't believe that to be true.

But Meera was always on her side, so perhaps, they

both needed the rest. If she woke up tomorrow morning with her best friend ready to take on the grunt work of the process before her, then she would know everything was all right. At least, she hoped it would be as she climbed the steps to reach Meera's side, and they headed up the curvature of them together.

Three weeks later

"I just don't understand why no one wants my bed and breakfast as a part from this town. It's frustrating, you know? I've worked my entire life to put my dreams aside, and the second I bring them to the forefront, I have to beg people to see their value." Not even my sister and best friend.

Sylvie let out a sigh as her therapist nodded along on the other end of their Skype call.

Her thick framed glasses were low on her nose as she studied Sylvie, waiting a couple of seconds before speaking. "Have you considered that the townspeople are not the enemies here?"

"What?"

"Bear with me here... What I'm getting at is the idea of problem shifting."

"Carol..."

She raised her hands up in surrender as Sylvie narrowed her eyes. "Here me out, Sylvie. These are people presenting a problem that you have no control over. That makes you feel angry, upset, maybe even hostile. Why?

Because you're reliving the trauma of a life you once knew. Is it possible that perhaps the problem isn't the townspeople, but still within you?"

Sylvie blinked at the screen in disbelief.

No, Carol, that wasn't the problem.

The townspeople being stuck in their ways and not wanting to change, so much so that she's being shunned by the monopoly of real-estate for the area—Ashton Housing—was the *problem*.

"Sylvie? Is that a fair assessment?" She pulled her glasses off her nose, watching Sylvie carefully, like she might jump out a window or commit a felony if she took her eyes from her.

Sylvie formed a heavy sigh that blew from her lips and puffed up her exasperated cheeks. She shrugged. "Sure. It could be."

"Well, this is usually when you shut down. It's the pattern. So, instead, I want you to take that bike ride we've been talking about. You got that bike, right?"

"Right."

"Yeah." She smiled sympathetically. "Go do that. Go for a bike ride, clear your thoughts, focus your breath, and then, we'll chat next week about how we can move forward."

"Okay." She barely spit out. Tears welled in her eyes, sprung from the tightening deep in her chest and the lump in her throat.

"Oh, and Sylvie, just before we end this call, make sure you focus on what you can control this week. Sound good?"

She forced herself to swallow as she nodded. "Good."

"All right, talk to you next Tuesday."

"Yep. Thanks, Carol." She didn't really mean to say thank you. It was a knee-jerk pleasantry. What she really wanted to say is, *why am I paying you hundreds of dollars every week to tell me that the only problem in my life is me?*

The call ended, and she shut her laptop, slinking out of bed and into the hallway, where it was quiet, and she figured both Lyla and Meera were probably working in their rooms. She pushed herself forward, not wanting to disturb their concentration to ask if they would want to go into town with her, and headed down the stairs.

The kitchen smelt like Chicken Divan, one of Lyla's specialties, baking in the oven for the day. It would no doubt be completely devoured by the three of them in the evening as they sat and watched a rom-com with a new bottle of wine.

This wasn't the vacation Meera had in mind when she mentioned it. But having just the women felt right given her current season. She felt more at home in Starwood than she had anywhere else for a long time. That had to mean something. It had to mean, she shouldn't give up.

The early evening air outside was warm and pleasant, a cool salty breeze whistled through the air as she wrapped her olive cardigan tighter around her. Her bike sat just at the bottom of the white wood porch steps. A wicker basket and silver belt fixed to the handlebars of the brown and cream bike. It looked like an old-fashioned 70s bike, like one she had as a tyke in New York.

"Hello." She smiled at it, though she had no desire to

bike that evening. Still, she knew it needed to happen. Carol was usually right, even when Sylvie wanted so desperately for her to be wrong. Perhaps, that's why biking seemed a better solution than actually thinking about her therapist's reflective questions.

She hopped on, grabbing her helmet from the basket and putting it on. After clicking the belt under her chin, she lifted the kickstand with the heel of her sneaker and turned toward the length of the driveway.

"Easy. Only my second time riding in the past few weeks. But it should be okay." She whispered to herself, not sure who she was trying to convince—the shifting winds or her nervous self. With a few wobbly pedals forward and quick jolts of the front wheel to keep from toppling over, she made her way down the sandy driveway.

Before long, she was pedaling with ease, the wind whipping past her ears and blowing her tresses around like streaks of golden brown in her peripherals. She could do this every day if she really committed to it, if it continued to shield her mind from thinking about the possibility of her dream ending before it had even begun.

As she rode up to the main town, she tried to keep her bike steady over the bumpy, uneven sidewalk. It was a hard feat, picket fences to her right and to her left a two lane street. She focused on the front tire, not wanting to go over too big a gap, lest she be thrown over the handlebars.

Her eyes were so intently homed in on the sidewalk, she collided with something tall and towering.

Her ribcage smashed into the hard metal handlebars, and her bike fell to the side before she could regain control. Just before she hit the cement, a hand grabbed the handlebars keeping them from rejecting her grip on them and tossing her into the street.

"Are you okay?" A warm voice like the setting sun asked, a slight alarm ringing behind its concern. Her eyes flitted about to see a beautiful man in a blue suit, legs partially under her bike, and strong hand holding her steady.

"I—did I?" Her mouth gaped in shock. "I hit you!"

She wriggled away in shock, falling to her knees before she forced herself up.

He rose with a chuckle, holding out his hand. "I think we hit each other."

"I'm so, so sorry. I don't normally ride bikes. It's really a pastime for me... I—it's just my—" Her words twisted over her tongue confusingly, not fully able to articulate her guilt. She was both attracted to this man and equally horrified at her clumsiness that her cheeks grew hot with embarrassment.

"It's quite all right. There's no need to fret. I'm fine." He looks over himself, then up and down her body, causing her heart to do a flip. "And you seem to be unharmed—"

"Yes, even so, I'm so sorry. I can pay you for any damage to your suit or shoes. They look expensive..." She glanced down at their shiny black leather, squinting to inspect them for any scuffs.

"No, seriously. I'm fine." He assured her, thick brows pulling together and up as his curved lips parted.

"I really feel awful, though." She bit her lip nervously as he picked up her bike for her.

"Are you hungry?"

She cocked her head at his question. "Uhm...a little, but—"

"Buy me dinner, and we'll call it a day." His smile was warm, inviting. He was practically oozing charm from every sharp angle of his perfect face.

"Oh, I..." She would have said no, really, she would. But she still felt horrible, and he looked very friendly. Perhaps, she could clear her guilty conscience by obliging, so she nodded, relenting. "Okay."

His grin grew even brighter as he waved a hand for her to walk in front of him, right toward the sweet and savory smells wafting from the diner down the street. She pushed her bike along as he stuck close to her side, greeting everyone who walked past them.

"Know a lot of people?" She crookedly grinned, and he softly chuckled.

"*Friends* with a lot of people."

"Hm." Her smile prevailed as they stepped up to a circular bike rack. He helped her lift the bike into a spot before guiding her up the steps. The sun had almost set by the time they stepped inside and found a seat in a booth at the front window.

Her sister and best friend would be worried if she wasn't back within the next half an hour. She was moments away from pulling her phone out of her pocket and texting or calling just to update them, but their server arrived just as she placed it atop the glossy wood table.

She watched as the man ordered for them both, requesting some special french toast. After the server left, she rested her chin in her hand, realizing that the feeling in the pit of her stomach had not gone away. His lips turned up at the corners as though he were intrigued by her.

"Welcome to town, by the way..." He implicitly elongated the last word.

"Oh, I'm Sylvia May Blythe." She blushed at her strange introduction of herself, giving her full unmarried name for the first time since the divorce. She shook her head. "But you can call Sylvie. And you are...?"

He stuck out his large, strong hand across the table, and she took it firmly as he introduced himself. "I'm Ronan." His ever-present grin grew a little wider. "Just Ronan."

Her lids dropped sarcastically. "Nice to meet you." She enunciated through an earnest smile that felt like an old friend.

"And you." His teeth shone brightly as the server delivered their drinks to the table, bowing out quickly as Sylvie's phone rang. Ronan's eyes were on it before hers were.

"Do you need to get that?"

"Oh." She looked down, knowing she probably had to or her sister would think the worst. "Do you mind? I'll just send her a text."

He shook his head, taking a sip of his water and settling back into his seat. After declining the call she quickly typed out a message.

"At the diner with a friend, pick me up in an hour?"

"Sorry about that." She placed her phone back onto the table, and he swatted a hand dismissively.

"I get it."

"My sister." Sylvie inhaled deeply, not sure where to begin. "She has this habit of worrying. She's younger than me, but always acts like she's older. I mean, it could be because she has everything together. Her whole life is picture-perfect. It's always been."

"Hm. And yours?"

"It might have been once. In fact, I thought coming here would be some sort of start for me—to make the picture pretty again." She rolled her straw wrapper into itself, twisting it. She wasn't sure why she was saying so much to this perfectly handsome stranger, but something about the way he leaned in when she spoke made her feel as though it were okay.

"It is a beautiful town." His soft smile reached his kind eyes as he studied her. She felt the ending of every nerve in her body, bending just slightly toward him. It made her heart skip and her stomach lift in this strange new way that it hadn't before.

Not in all her forty-seven years had someone this magnetic crossed her path. He was as equally charming as he was alluring, soft yet strong and confident. She didn't know where to place him in her mind because there wasn't a space for someone like him. At least, that's what she thought—that he was too good to be true.

The food was served, but he continued to prompt her with questions. Though she tried to play coy, she ended up divulging her struggles with the town and how everything felt hopeless.

"The entire town is against my starting a bed and breakfast. I can't even get Ashton Housing to return my calls. It's like I'm on their blacklist, and I'm being shunned for even considering my own happiness. I get it, you know? A big-city lady coming to a small town to start a business, but I want to avoid doing anything to disturb the quaintness. I only wish to add to it."

He nodded as he took a bite of his French toast, which smelt like the perfect balance of sweet and spice. Cinnamon and maple swirled between them, and her stomach growled, longing to divulge in its delectable flavor palate, but she couldn't stop herself long enough to take a bite.

"It's just ridiculous that this Ashton place is basically a dictator. A bully even. I just can't imagine why a business like that wouldn't want to consider what I'm proposing."

He covered his mouth, raising a finger as his brows pulled together. She took the opportunity to take her first mouth-watering bite. It was everything she could ever dream of in a French toast. Crispy, soft, buttery. Then sweet, cinnamon spice, and all of these other bits of warmth and goodness mixed in that she couldn't quite pinpoint.

"Good?" He breathed a laugh through his nose as she closed her eyes and nodded, taking in the moment so at least if everything else went wrong, this could be something to fondly remember. "Good."

Admiration spilled from the creases of his eyes to his pink lips. Why couldn't she stop staring at his mouth?

"So, about this Ashton housing situation and why they aren't returning calls—"

"Oh, I'll tell you why! They're power hungry, Ronan. It's as simple as that. Why else would they be the only real estate company in the entire area? I bet—"

"Ronan!" A gentleman in his mid-twenties approached the table with a young woman on his arm. They beamed excitedly as they shook his hand.

"Ash." He nodded to them. "Mary. Great to see you both."

"We're sorry to interrupt. We just wanted to thank you again for helping us close that deal on our dream home last week. It truly was a miracle."

"Oh, it's honestly an honor to help you get your first home. Those are always my favorite deals."

"Ronan Ashton, your father would be proud to see the man you've become."

Ashton? Sylvie's vision spun and that feeling at the pit of her stomach curdled into a mess. This was not happening. She had not just foiled any chance she had at salvaging her dreams.

CHAPTER 3

Home Is Where Her Heart Is

Ronan couldn't be the actual Ashton Housing... This was some misunderstanding, and it would all make sense soon enough, at least she hoped. He turned back toward her as the couple left, and the check arrived at the table.

Her fingers fumbled for the card in the back of her phone case, but he grabbed the check before she could reach it, tucking money into the clipboard.

"It's on me." He pulled out a black card from inside his navy suit and slid it across the table. "Give me a call." He nodded with a soft smile that reached his knowing eyes as she looked down at the card in disbelief and read, *Ashton Housing*.

Either this man was insane for wanting to help her, or he had some ulterior motive that she could not pinpoint at that very moment.

"Oh my goodness, Sylvia! You scared Meera and I."

Lyla's voice pulled Sylvie from her trance, and she looked up to see them both gawking at her.

"Who was that man?" Meera asked with quiet excitement, clearly never doubting her friend's ability to keep herself safe in a virtually crime-free town.

"And what was he doing buying you dinner?" Lyla's stance was angry, but her words were still laced with intrigue.

"I'll talk about it at home. Can we go?"

Layla leered at her for a moment, considering if this was worth letting go. Sylvie glanced at Meera for help, who grabbed Lyla's arm and tugged gently.

"Yes, let's head back." She pleaded a little, and Lyla pouted her lips to the side.

"Fine." Lyla finally sighed and turned on her heel as Sylvie stood with a breathy laugh.

Meera pinched her side gently as they exited the diner and whispered, "It's nice to see that smile back. I missed it."

They headed down the steps, and Sylvie nudged Meera's shoulder affectionately before grabbing her bike off the rack and sliding it into the back seat of Lyla's car.

On the drive back, it was fairly quiet, which only made way for Sylvie to think about the things she'd rather not. It wasn't just the fact that some stranger had bought her dinner and listened to her woes. It was that her woes were about that said stranger and had she known this very vital piece of information, she would have never divulged such details.

Then, there was his dreamy charm and the look in his

eyes when he listened to her. She could have said the sky was green, and he would have nodded along, studying her as though he were trying to see things through her skewed eyes. It was adolescent, the way the pit of her stomach still fluttered at the thought of him. That made her apprehensive to share anything with the girls, should they discover her odd feelings underneath the pure embarrassment of the entire ordeal.

After arriving at their rental home, the three women made their way inside, a silent tension growing as they neared the door. Sylvie could sense their gazes on her, waiting for her to spill everything like a brimming glass. She did feel like a brimming glass, but for many other reasons that she couldn't explain, nor did she want to just yet.

"I'm going to bed. I am utterly exhausted." She forced a yawn, not looking back at the two as she lumbered up the steps. They were still treating her like she was fragile, and perhaps, she was. But that small sensitivity was to her benefit tonight because neither of them pushed her to speak. She was happy with it that way, at least for tonight.

In the morning, it was a different story with the girls. Breakfast was served with questions and concerns, all aimed at the man they had seen paying for her meal and abruptly leaving. After a night of tossing and turning, ruminating on it with distress and need for input, she was already in a state that didn't allow for her to put it off any longer. So, instead of fighting them on it, she divulged the entire incident.

Every detail that made her cringe about how she had

basically insulted him to his face, and how he didn't even seem the least bit thrown. The girls were hooked, barely taking bites of the savory omelet Meera had made for them.

"So, he just got up and left?" Lyla scrunched her nose and took a sip of her freshly squeezed orange juice.

Sylvie grimaced and pressed a palm to her forehead in distress. "Yes."

Meera reached for her arm comfortingly. "This sounds like it could be a good thing, right? I mean, you'll call him."

Sylvie pulled a face at Meera's words.

Meera tilted her chin, brows lowering. "You're not going to call him?"

"I don't know. It seems too good to be true. If I accept his help, he might want to dictate the project or—"

"There might not be a project without his help, Sylvie," Lyla asserted, causing Sylvie to pause.

"You both think I should call this man?"

They nodded vigorously, and she shifted her jaw.

"If you don't want to, you don't have to, though." Meera studied her earnestly.

Lyla cocked her head, a scowl overtaking her usually soft features. "What do you mean? She needs to call him. This is the entire reason we came here. If she doesn't, we're basically wasting our time."

"Sylvie has every right to choose how she goes about this. No one is forcing you to be here, so if you don't like the way she's going about things, you can just leave," Meera snapped back.

"Oh, really?" She tilted her head, pale yellow curls bobbing with her offense.

"Really. I think you should leave if you're going to try to control everything about everyone like you always do, Lala. We're here for Sylvie, or have you forgotten that?"

Lyla scrunched her nose, about to add injury to the insult already creating a nervous hostility.

"Okay, both of you, stop. I'll call him, okay? You're both right. I'll call him right now."

Both Meera and Lyla's frames sundered from one another, sinking slowly down into their seats as though she had found their off button.

"I'll be back." She informed them before grabbing her phone and heading out to the porch.

The air smelt like summer for the first time since their arrival, though it was still spring, and she enjoyed the warm salty air filling her lungs. She pulled the card out of her wallet on the back of her phone case, turning it over in her hand just once before dialing Ronan's number.

It only rang three times before he answered. "Sylvie?"

She was taken aback by his immediate recognition of her. "Y-yes. How did you know?"

"I have *a lot* of friends, remember. All of them are saved to my phone. But not your number. I'll do that right now."

"Does that make me a friend then, Ronan?"

"Suppose it does, Sylvie." She could hear the smile in his warm voice, and she couldn't help but reciprocate it, feebly attempting not to get swept up in the pleasantries. She had to stay on topic, had to know if he was willing to help her or if this was just a way to punish her for insulting his family's business. "So, about this bed and breakfast..."

"Yes, firstly, I'm so sorry for last night, I had no idea. It was wrong of me to just vent like that to a complete and total stranger."

"Sylvie, it's quite all right. I genuinely understand. Passion is not something I lack. It's why I love this business, and it's why I'm more than willing to help you."

She couldn't believe his words, couldn't comprehend her luck. She had never been very lucky, at least not for a long time. But this day she was pot-of-gold-at-the-end-of-the-rainbow, field-full-of-four-leaf-clovers kind of lucky. Her heart raced at the possibilities of his help bringing her dreams to fruition, everything she had wanted for so long.

"Ronan, that's beyond kind of you. I just assumed that when your company didn't respond to me, they were against this whole idea."

"Well, they were, but I held a meeting this morning right after talking to the mayor."

"The mayor?"

"Yes. I had to get building permits if we're going to build on one of the spots available for you."

"Building permit..." she trailed quietly, astounded by the paradigm shift her world had taken in just the past few moments.

"Yeah, actually, I have some time set aside today to

bring you around to the building locations. Would you be available if I picked you up in about half an hour?"

She didn't check the time to respond yes before she gave him her address, and they were saying their goodbyes. Her heart was still pounding when she hung up the phone, and she grabbed onto the front window to steady herself.

The door burst open as Lyla and Meer flanked to either side of her, helping her sit down on the porch swing and fanning her as she blinked between them.

"What happened?" Meera asked, sitting next to her, as Lyla continued to fan frantically.

"I'm getting the bed and breakfast."

"What does that mean?" Lyla asked, still frantic, before Sylvie reached her hand up and caught her arm.

"Ronan got approval to build me a bed and breakfast."

"There's no catch?" She asked, and Meera glared up at her.

Sylvie shook her head. "No. I have to get ready."

She shot up, brushing past Lyla, who appeared far more concerned about this news than Meera.

"There's a sundress in my closet, Sylvie." She called after her with a grin as Sylvie frantically rushed up the stairs and straight to Meera's room. A beautiful robin egg blue dress waited for her right where Meera had said. Thin straps, buttons down the length of the a-line mid-maxi dress. This was her color and size, not Meera's, so she knew she had bought it for her as a gift.

She shook her head as she carefully pulled it off the hanger and slipped it on, heading to the bathroom immediately after. The morning light streamed through the windows above the shower, casting streams of golden sunlight throughout her tangled waves. She fought with them for a bit, spraying them down and dousing them with water, before finally being satisfied with their level of messiness.

After covering her lips with berry-colored gloss and curling her dark lashes, she slathered on some sunscreen and headed back down the steps, where her white sandals awaited her.

"You look incredible." Meera peeped her head around the corner, a cup of coffee in hand, and she looked Sylvie up and down in awe.

"You are too nice, Meera." She turned to her, pulling her into a hug. "Thank you for the dress."

"Of course. I thought you needed something to encapsulate the new life you've found for yourself."

Sylvie's eyes welled up, but a knock on the door broke them both apart and forced her to pull it together.

"Good luck." Meera whispered as Sylvie took a gentle breath and strode toward the door. When she opened it, her efforts to stay calm were thwarted. Her chest tightened at the sight of Ronan's glowing frame in the doorway, squeezing every ounce of air out of her.

"Good morning." He grinned that brilliant, bright smile of his, and she softly nodded, unable to speak just yet. The sleeves of his white button up were rolled to his elbow, exposing his muscular forearms as he waved to Meera.

"Morning." She chimed before giving Sylvie a quick

glance that held a thousand meanings and bobbing back into the kitchen pleasantly.

"Should we get going?" His timber voice asked, stepping aside, so she could see his car parked in the wide driveway.

"Yes." She managed to get out with another gentle nod as she forced herself to avoid looking at him, so her nerves would dissipate. Her sandals collided with the soft sand as he pulled the car door open for her, and her pounding heart softened a bit as she thanked him, sliding into the car. She had to focus on her dream, not Ronan, she reminded herself as he crossed to his side of the car and got in.

"All right, so three locations are available. I was thinking we would start with the closest and then work our way to the others?"

"Okay. Yes." She glanced at him while trying to keep her thoughts far from the dazzling depth behind his pine blue eyes. As they pulled away from her rental home, she envisioned what her life would look like, running this bed and breakfast. She couldn't help but dream up her life without any pain, the way this type of thinking would eventually bring her, in the past. Before, she could only hope that one day she might get lost in her ideas without them reminding her of their impossibility. But now, everything felt possible for her.

They pulled up to the first lot, but it didn't encapsulate her vision. It was in the center of town, where an abandoned office had been demolished due to structural damage. They spoke only briefly about it with the landowner as they walked around in the rubble of bricks and mortar before heading back to the car.

"It's not right." She shook her head when Ronan asked her what she thought. There was a part of her that felt nervous telling him how she felt about it, but he only smiled when she did.

"Good thing we have other options." He glanced over at her, and she grinned back as they continued on to the next property.

"You're too nice. Has anyone ever told you that?" She spoke up when only the sound of the engine and heart beating in her ears filled the space between them.

"Can anyone ever be *too nice*?" He cocked his brow, pressing the tip of his tongue to his top lip.

"I think so."

"I don't. And you know what, Sylvia May? I'm going to prove it to you." She didn't know what that meant or why he was so sure of her being wrong, but she enjoyed his company.

So, often she found that the people placed in her life were one's that she needed to learn from. As if they all watered her in a way that forced her to grow. She hoped that she could do that for the people closest to her—be a watering can. But what could she possibly learn from Ronan?

She knew very little about him thus far, except that he was willing to bend over backward to help someone who basically spit in his face less than twenty-four hours ago.

They came to a stop in front of the next area. This time it was a clearing just past the town, but it was too far from the water—a beachfront was most ideal. They walked around the space a little, trudging through the tall grass and underneath shady trees. He held his hand to help her many times, but she didn't take it until she nearly tripped over a rotten log. It was there, so she grabbed it, and bumps rose along her arm upon touching his skin.

It was the falling that nearly caused her to twist an ankle that had caused the chills, she told herself. That was all.

"So?" Ronan's steady hand was still clasped around hers as she took one more survey of the area.

"Not quite right." She shook her head, pursing her lips.

"So, what is right?" He took a heart thumping step closer to her. "What does Sylvia May dream about?"

She swallowed the knot in her throat and looked past him before her eyes caught his. "The beach."

His parted lips pressed together, curing up at the edges as he pulled her back toward the car.

"Where are we going?" She chuckled at his abrupt shift.

"To the final location."

They headed further out of the area, just on the edge of town. The road was bumpy like cobblestone and shook the car as they rolled over it and up a small hill. After stopping, Sylvie got out of the car, instantly met by the sound of the ocean. Past a towering tree-line, there was an open space of wavy grass taller than her hips. As they approached the clearing, the curvature of the ocean meeting the sky lifted in the horizon.

The closer they got, the easier she could grasp where they were.

It looked to be a private beach, just below the hill. To the left was a steeper hill, adjacent to theirs, on top of which was a beautiful white lighthouse, pointing out to the wild ocean below.

Everything within her soared, and her lips parted as she took in the beauty of it all. This felt like home to her, she could sense the land's significance under her feet as she lifted her chin to the billowing clouds slowly passing overhead.

A deep breath of relief and excitement filled her..

"This is it," she whispered, not wanting to disturb the majestic sounds swirling through the briny breeze.

"This is it?" He repeated, his words low and curved.

"Yes." She looked out at the water as she spoke, so sure of this decision. Perhaps more sure of anything than she had ever been in her entire life.

"All right, that leaves one more thing to show you."

She pivoted toward him as he pulled his phone out of his back pocket and turned the screen to her. His finger flicked through stunning sketches of a home she had only seen in bits and pieces when she closed her eyes. Her eyes widened as he continued to show her the entirety of the bed and breakfast that would be built where they stood.

"This is magnificent," she breathed. "When did you have time to do this?"

"Last night. I stayed up. I just couldn't shake our conversation or the passion that you had—have. It's admirable. To be honest, I can't remember the last time I felt something so deeply, and it got me thinking."

"You make art to help you think?"

He waved a hand. "This isn't really art. But, I'll accept the compliment." His eyes danced between hers, and for a moment, she forgot what they were even doing. He really was very kind.

There was so much to discover about him, so much she wanted to know, but she couldn't let herself get distracted. This was a business partnership now, that's all it could be. If she made one wrong move, he might call the whole thing off. And she was unable to risk that type of repercussion, not when she was entirely too close to her heart's desire.

His expression changed as she forced her eyes away from him, and he quickly shoved his phone in his pocket, staring out at the ocean with her for a moment.

"We'll break ground on Monday." He cut their tension in half, glanced at her sideways with his bright eyes. Her heart leapt out of her chest, and she almost lurched to grab it, had it not have made her look insane. She already decided that they couldn't complicate things, so sticking to that was essential.

"Great, so should we head back now?" She turned toward the car, but he caught her wrist before she could stray too far. The maneuver made her unsteady on her feet, and she nearly lost her balance, had he not slid his hand to the small of her back. Her sharp breath caught in the wind, and she looked up at him, terrified of losing control.

"Are you okay?" He spoke soft and low, she only

nodded, not stopping until he took a breath to speak again. "Our first date didn't go so well."

"Date?" She chuffed sarcastically, brows going tall.

"Yes. Our first. I asked you, I paid. It was a date."

"Definitely not."

"Which part?" His grin went crooked, and a charming flame of mischief lit behind his intent eyes.

"I'm not doing this, Ronan." She tried to warn him, but his arms were still around her and the warmth of him made her unsteady.

"Sylvie, I'm asking if you'll go on a date with me." She took a breath to speak, but he lifted his chin to object to her obstinance. "And before you say no, I promise that it will be the best date you have ever gone on."

Sylvie's heart would have gone into overdrive if it was still in her chest. So much for not complicating anything...

CHAPTER 4
Brake To Start

T he drive home was silent but not uncomfortable. She hadn't given Ronan an answer after he had asked her to go out with him. How could she not respond?

Had she not already determined that she would not mix business with pleasure? She had lived far too long to give in to such frivolous temptations. Yet, her lips wouldn't solidify her decision, so he answered for her.

"I'll give you time to think about it," he had said, as though she wasn't capable of putting her foot down right then and there.

Country music played in the background, and she could feel him glance at her the entire drive back to her rental home. Every time he did so, her stomach tied itself in another knot. That meant about twelve were congregating within her.

Perhaps, the problem wasn't that she didn't want to go

on a date with him; rather, she did. She was attracted to him. No denying that. It wasn't just looks, either.

Despite the opposition in the town he had grown up in, he took a chance in helping her. That was admirable, alluring like the charm he exuded with little effort. But was saying yes to him worth risking everything?

That she was not certain of, at least not as certain as she was before he properly asked her on a date.

Before she realized it, they were at her home, and he had parked that car. Was he wanting to have some sort of conversation now? Her mind couldn't take another second of thinking and reasoning, rationalizing and worrying. So, she practically leapt out of the car, speed-walking toward her home as he called after her.

"You forgot your phone."

She froze, turning her head to see her phone in his hand. He smiled, but his brows pulled together, creasing in his forehead. She jogged back to the car in response, cheeks flushing with embarrassment as she grabbed it and ran back to the house. His chuckled dance on top of the wind as she opened her door and slid inside.

As his tires rolled out of the driveway, she leaned back against the door with a heavy breath. That was far too close and far too humiliating. Time to lock herself away for the night, but the house was too dark inside. Her hand instinctively reached for the light-switch and just as she caught it, every light flickered on.

"Surprise!!!" Meera and Lyla shouted in unison—the most unified they had ever been. They held a bottle of champagne together, kaleidoscope-colored party hats donned their heads, and their eyes were lit with excitement.

"What's this?" Sylvie blinked, hand on her chest.

"We wanted to congratulate you for choosing a property for your bed and breakfast!" Meera exclaimed.

"How did you know?"

Lyla wiggled the champagne. "We went into town today, and heard some woman chanting outside the town hall building."

"What?" Sylvie's heart sank a little. She knew the town had been opposed to her ideas, but not enough to start a rally.

Meera shook her head, brows tall. "Yes, apparently she was not happy about the mayor's decision to grant you a piece of land."

"Was there a large crowd?" Sylvie gulped the knot forming in her throat as she walked past them and into the kitchen to sit down. They followed quietly, pausing for a little too long after she had asked.

"Numerous people were gathered," Meera finally said, earning her a sharp glare from Lyla.

"It's fine, Sylvie. I'm sure when they see it all finished, they'll be glad the mayor approved the build."

Sylvie wanted to believe her sister, but her words were not as assuring as she'd desperately wanted them to be. She rested her chin in her hands as Meera uncorked the champagne, grabbing the flute glasses already set out on the tiled countertop. They clinked together as she tipped the foamy gold drink into them.

It was quiet for too long before she handed them out,

and Lyla let out a dramatic sigh. Both Sylvie and Meera looked at her then back to their glasses before she did it again.

"Is everything okay, Lyla?" Meera blinked her round brown eyes with annoyance.

"Well, I guess. I just wish we could hear more about hunky-dory, who you spent the entire day with." She pointed her words at Sylvie, who took a larger sip of champagne than she usually did. It stung her eyes, fizzy bubbles popping around her cheeks and nose as she tipped the glass.

"Ooo, yes." Meera leaned over the countertop toward Sylvie.

"I—I don't know. There isn't much to discuss. He is really kind for doing this, and I appreciate his *professional* help."

"*Professional*." Lyla enunciated, taking a sip of her champagne, elbow resting on her arm across her stomach.

"Yes. He and I are in business together. All that happened today was a part of our business plans." Aside from him asking her on a date, she decisively decided to leave that part out. It would only prove Lyla right, and she already displayed too smug a look for Sylvie's liking.

"Well, I think that's really lovely, Sylvie," Meera chimed in, breaking their tense stare-down and raising a glass. "To dreams coming true, *business* flourishing, and also, to Sylvie."

The girls raised their glasses and clanked them together, settling down in stools around the kitchen counter, gabbing about the day and what was to come for all of them. It was a sweet moment of connectivity. Mostly because Sylvie felt that sense of peace she had long awaited for since first learning about her divorce.

Life was moving forward, and maybe, it had always been, but now, she could see it. Like watching the sun set, she finally felt a breath of calm when it disappeared behind the horizon.

"So, Monday, seven a.m.?" Meera asked when Lyla had gotten up to make a tipsy call to her husband in the other room.

"Yeah." Sylvie grinned into her empty glass before catching her friend's dark amber eyes.

"You really don't have any feelings for Ronan? None at all?" Her friend knew her too well to really be asking that question. All she was doing was observing Sylvie's awareness of her feelings.

Sylvie knew her friend just as well, so she was sure this was why Meera had asked again.

"Even if I feel anything for him beyond simple intrigue, nothing can ever happen between us. It's too risky. I should stick to the project only."

"That's a good idea." Was all Meera could say before Lyla came back into the room, insisting they watch a classic movie on the small tv in the living room.

"Please, *Gone With The Wind* is the greatest movie of all time." She tugged at both Meera and Sylvie's hands until they chuckled, relenting to her wishes, even though they both knew she would be out before during the first half of the movie.

Not twenty minutes in, as predicted, Lyla was curled

up under a heap of blankets on the couch opposite to Sylvie and Meera.

"I should go to sleep." Sylvie whispered to Meera, who nodded with a yawn.

"Me, too," she whispered back and followed Sylvie quietly up the stairs.

They parted ways at their bedroom, saying goodnight, though Sylvie could sense Meera wanted to say more. She may have endeavored to carry on the conversation regarding Ronan. But ultimately, it was, as she said—a good idea to focus on the tasks at hand. None of which included accepting his invitation to a date. Even if it was with Ronan. Even if he had promised, it would be the best she'd ever been on.

As she lay in bed that night, she stared at the ceiling fan for a long time, watching the patterns it cast on the walls as the moonlight streamed in through the open window.

She loved sleeping with the window open; she had always done it when she was on vacation. But in New York, you'd be daft to leave your window even ajar in the evening—for a multitude of reasons. It was safe in Starwood, though. Everything was, even the air that filtered in from the expanse of towering trees, carried atop the constant sea breeze.

Just before this lulled her to sleep, she sent out a message to her children:

"I've secured a property in Starwood, Massachusetts, and we'll be breaking ground on Monday for the beachside bed and breakfast. I love you all and hope I didn't scare anyone too much when I took off after the divorce."

She sat her phone back on her bedside, falling asleep with a smile for the first time in many years.

The entirety of the weekend flew by. Most of it was spent heading to towns further into the mainland to grab new clothes. None of the girls had planned to stay in Massachusetts for this long, and they were beginning to run out of basic things as the weather shifted into summer. Sunday night was spent packing lunches for herself and the girls. Sylvie knew they would enjoy what she had prepped, setting hers aside in the fridge and heading upstairs to bed.

As she lay down that night, focusing on steady breathing to help her fall asleep, her phone chimed on her nightstand, lighting up the entire room with a bluish-white glow. She turned over, grabbing it and unlocking the screen without getting a chance to see who had messaged her.

The phone pulled up her messages, and there she saw who had reached out to her. Ronan. She tapped on the message with the tip of her finger, squinting at the screen to read it.

"I'll pick you up in the morning, 6:30 a.m."

Her brows creased together as she puffed air through the side of her mouth. This was complicated. If she said yes, they would be forced to spend nonwork time together every morning and evening. On the other hand, if she said no, it would seem like she was avoiding him without cause. Her therapist had reminded her the other day that '*no*' was a full sentence. She had heard that somewhere before, but even then, it didn't help her muster enough courage to utilize it.

So, she typed back, *"Actually, I've been trying to get my workout's in..."*

She grimaced at the lie before continuing to type.

"And, I've decided to ride my bike to the site tomorrow. Thanks anyway. See you at 7 a.m., sharp."

After hitting send, she reviewed it anxiously as the dot dot dots let her know he was typing back.

"7 a.m. sharp."

She quickly set her alarm for four thirty, knowing the bike ride would be a rather arduous one. With one last shake of her head, she laid her phone face down on her nightstand before shutting her eyes and forcing sleep to come.

The alarm blared loudly, she thought something horrible was happening—a fire, a storm warning, an earthquake. Her room was dark with the early blue light of a barely risen sun. She reached over and turned her phone over, tapping the screen with barely opened eyes until the alarm stopped assaulting her ears.

With a brief stretch and yawn, her feet hit the cold wood floors, and she was sliding out of bed, crossing to the bathroom to put on the clothes she had set out the night before. It was a brown jumpsuit with wooden buttons that she had found at one of the thrift shops in Nantucket.

Meena had promised to braid her hair in the morning, but her morning wasn't supposed to have started this early, so she knew her friend wouldn't be awake just yet. Instead, she pulled her hair back into a low bun, leaving a few stray pieces around her face, and tied an off-white bandana over it all.

After tip-toeing downstairs, she grabbed her lunch and water bottle out of the fridge, slipped on her white sneakers at the door, and headed out to her bike with sleep still in the corners of her hazel eyes.

The morning sun had just peeked over the treelike, and the sky was a vibrant array of majestic colors, swirling between sweeping white clouds. She moved across the sandy driveway with purpose and tossed her things into the wicker basket of her bike before hopping on it.

With her helmet secured, she pushed off. It was shaky, as her starts usually were, but it evened out by the time she hit the main road. She was always good with directions and knew what street to follow and turn down to reach her destination. So, she pedaled quickly, pushing herself to her limits as the sun slowly rose behind her.

That same rush of a perfect mixture between peace and adrenaline pumped through her veins as she clutched tightly to the rubber handles, expectancy brimming in her chest. Today was the true beginning of everything, and she couldn't wait to see it come to life in front of her eyes. Nothing about her life before this was ever horrible. In fact, raising her four children was the highlight of her life. But they hadn't needed her for a long time, not the way they used to.

This was her baby, her newest addition to the highs and lows of life. It represented every struggle and win she had ever gone through or achieved. That alone was enough to cause elation, and she used those feelings to push her forward as she pedaled with adamant consistency.

As the sun fixed at the apex of the bright blue sky, she was still pedaling, sweat dripping down every part of her as she persisted. She didn't have the balance or hand-eye coordination to check the time, but she could tell she was late. She also knew that she still had a ways to go before she would reach the property.

Dread set in as sweat accumulated in the worst places, dripping down her back, behind her knees, and her palms that gripped tightly to the handle bars. Breathing with every heave of her foot, she turned down the last street leading to the property site.

Fifteen minutes later, she had finally arrived to a surplus of workers in white hard hats, holding backhoes, shovels, and handling heavy machinery to lay down the foundation. Her heart raced with anticipation as the swell of excitement overtook her. The foundation of her dreams was coming to fruition right before her eyes. She tossed off her helmet and worked to regain a normal breathing pattern as she strode toward it.

Slowly, she headed up the hill; the sea breeze cooled off her hot damp skin as she stopped at the top of the hill. A figure in the distance seemed to notice her, and as they approached, revealing a very muscular, shirtless man, body glistening in the sun like a GQ model. Her breath stopped short once she saw just who it was.

"Ronan." She waved, calling with a shaky voice that might not have even been heard because of the winds bristling between them. His legs swished through the tall grass until he stood in front of her, sweat rolling down his torso. He offered her a mouth-parted grin, a crease in his forehead as he sighed a heavy breath.

"That, uh…" He flicked up his wrist with a black rubber watch. "7 a.m. *sharp* ended up being rather *dull*, Sylvia May."

She sucked in her lips with a slow nod. "About that…"

"No need to explain." He raised a hand nonchalantly, lips still curled up at the corners. "Let's get started on some things for the house."

"I'm going to help with the build?" He grabbed her hand to gently guide her, and her stomach did a flip.

"Sort of." He chuckled before looking back at her, eyes trailing her up and down, making her hold her breath before he shook his head. "Don't worry, though. No one's giving you power tools."

He handed her a hard hat at the end of their walk, and they crossed to one of the sections of the building site. Ronan glanced back at her studying gaze as workers hustled around them.

"Here." He reached into the tool belt around his waist and pulled out a flat head screwdriver. She looked at it for a moment, uncertain of what he wanted her to do. He breathed a laugh at her apprehension, taking a step closer to her and reaching for her hand. Chills rose as he did this —a response like little pricks of metal clinging to a magnet. He was a magnet, that was why she was feeling this way. That's what she told herself.

When their hands collided, Sylvie blinked at the

shockwave he had caused as it traveled through her very core.

"I'm not very skilled with tools..." She trailed off, feeling embarrassed for speaking because her words sounded far-off and dream-like. He softly smiled in response, sliding the tool into her hand, so gently she barely noticed it until he was guiding her forward.

Then, her heart raced at a speed she hadn't known it could and didn't think it would when she saw just where he was leading her.

CHAPTER 5

True North

"I thought you said I wouldn't be operating heavy machinery." Sylvie's eyes grew round as she saw the towering excavator, seeming to gain height the closer they inched toward it.

"You won't be." Ronan assured her as he led her up the steps. She gawked at him like he was insane, and her knees began to lock. Nothing in her wanted him to push her any further. She barely knew how to ride a bike without wreaking havoc on herself and others. How was she supposed to operate this giant death trap? "I promise, you don't have to worry, Sylvia May."

Her hesitancy was no secret, especially not when she looked down at him from the second step. He only squeezed her hand reassuringly and gestured her up with a gentle tip of his chin.

"Trust me." He softly ordered, piney irises toggling between hers. She could give him a million reasons why that was a horrible thing to say to her. Why trusting people had been something she always struggled with, for reasons she didn't want to think about. But instead, she sucked in salty air that burned her nostrils and twisted back around, finishing her walk up to the long seat inside the excavator.

Ronan followed her and took the center seat, patting the space beside him for her to join. She turned the screwdriver over in her hand as he started up the vehicle, wondering what this could possibly be for. As the machine inched forward, positioning where the men in hard hats ordered Ronan, she watched his strong hands expertly maneuver it.

She was shocked by the fact that he even knew how to operate something like this. Especially considering the fact that he had inherited his family business and probably never needed to work like this a day in his charmed life.

Just as they came to a stop in front of blue wires taut between wood sticks in the ground, he looked over at her, brows tall. "Ready?"

"For what?" She asked just as he reached for one of her hands and brought it over to one of the black shiny knobs on a metal pole sticking up from the dashboard.

"You're going to break ground." He answered her right as he shoved the knob forward with her hand. The bucket, with pointy teeth at the end of the yellow metal arm, plummeted to the ground and scooped up a clump of wispy lime grass and dark crumbly soil.

The machine pivoted nearly 180 degrees, dropping the contents onto the grass behind them. After Ronan guided the machine back to its original position, he turned the key, and the loud rumbling noises stopped.

Below, the men cheered and clapped, though Sylvie wasn't sure why. She looked at Ronan, and he grinned, joining the clapping.

"Congratulations, Sylvia May, you just broke ground on Starwood's very first bed and breakfast." He held out his hand to help her down, and she grabbed it with her free one, squeezing the screwdriver in her other.

They stepped down to the ground once more, and the team returned to work, backing up a cement truck as someone took their place in the excavator. She didn't realize Ronan was still holding her hand until the pit of her stomach clenched and the skin on the backs of her arms flooded with chills. Immediately, she slipped her hand from his, turning toward the construction beginning to really take way.

He didn't say anything to her, and she couldn't tell what he was thinking as he looked over the site with her. A bulldozer came in next, taking part in flattening out the land and making the earth shake beneath their feet. Most of the afternoon, they watched, trying to stay out of the way as Ronan occasionally referenced the blueprint to instruct people. After a few hours, the concrete truck backed into a spot, pouring fresh concrete into a marked area.

"Come." Ronan motioned for her to follow him after he had taken off toward the gray sludge pile of slowly hardening concrete. She followed him, avoiding the workers buzzing past her on all sides, stopping when they reached the edge of the wet concrete.

"What are we doing?" She scrunched her nose at the

scent as Ronan grinned back at her. His lips curled at the edges playfully, that forced her to look down at the screwdriver still in her hand.

"You're craving your initials in the foundation." He reached for her to take his hand, but she avoided it, ignoring her heart beating in her ears, stepping past him and crouching down to the concrete. She reached forward, and it was as if she could sense all the lives she was about to touch. All the people she would be able to care for, share her love with, every new memory was going to be held by this strong foundation. Her very initials would mark it as so, solidifying it as the foundation hardened like a permanent fixture of her dreams coming to life.

Slowly, she touched the tip of the screwdriver down and wrote out her initials.

"SMB"

"It looks perfect." Ronan held his hand out to help her up as she turned around, but she didn't take it, more adamant now more than ever to not let him get under her skin. This needed to stop—the strange pull between them like the inevitable rising tide behind her.

He didn't seem the least bit offset by her avoidance of him as he smiled down at her signature. They stepped away as another group of men came in with tools to work on something related to the foundation that Sylvie has no idea about.

Most of the day, she had to remain by Ronan's side, and it didn't help that he was shirtless for it all.

"Help me with this land marker, Sylvie?" he asked when the sun was starting to lower in the late afternoon.

Sweat dripped down their backs. She could see his and feel hers as they stepped further from the booming noises of construction workers carrying on with their jobs.

"How far out are we marking?"

"Well, right now, we just need to show the pipe layers where their lines have to cross with the town's."

"Not that I know anything about building a house, but shouldn't that have already been done?"

"It should have, but every so often we have to make do with unexpected disturbances in workflow. It's not an exact science every time. I've got the water guys coming tomorrow, and there should be a spray paint marker somewhere down here..." He trailed looking around in the grass, turning in circles as he narrowed his eyes at the ground. She searched the area around him as he went off with his wooden stick in another direction. As she took another few steps, she saw the neon orange paint in the distance, nearing glowing in the sunlight.

"There!" she called, and he whipped around, jogging to where she had pointed without even getting a good look.

"Where?" he asked, continuing and sincerely believing that she was telling the truth. She liked that about him, admired it, even. But this wasn't about him; they were working. She shook her head, honey brown hair twisting around her body, before answering him.

"By the tree," she shouted, and his eyes scanned the area as he came to a brisk walk before discovering what she had been referring to. He gave her thumbs up before stopping in front of it and shoving the steak into the ground.

"Done." He clapped, running back up the slight hill of tall grass until he nearly collided with her. "Let's head back."

He lifted his chin, exposing the ripple of his neck, connecting with his muscular shoulders, and she forced herself to turn around, so she didn't continue down any further. She thought she heard him snicker to himself as they walked back, but then again, it was rather windy. It must have been the grass swiping together, she thought— she hoped.

Throughout the course of the day, she found herself lingering, her eyes wandering, her heart racing. Even when she didn't want to, she defied herself. Her entire body reacted to him like mentos in soda. It was a chemical reaction that somehow couldn't be reversed, prohibited, or avoided. Frustrating, to say the least, and to say the most, she was one more flirty look away from running as fast as she could into the ocean and swimming to another continent.

As the sun was setting, all the day's excitements and confusions mixed and melded like the colors in the sky, and Sylvie was too tired to try to resolve it. That's why when Ronan asked her if he could drive her home, she agreed. After all, she couldn't stomach another ride like the one this morning. It was far too arduous, especially after the day she had under the hot sun.

"All right," she conceded, and he cocked his head, brows raised like he couldn't believe she said yes so easily. It must have been what he was thinking because it's the way she felt when she answered him.

"All right?" he repeated.

"Yes. You can drive me home." She spoke nonchalantly, but her heartbeat gave her away as she joined his side. They trekked to his truck parked at the side of the road. They were about to reach it when he turned, eyes glued to something for a moment before he moved toward it wordlessly.

"Ronan?" she called, squinting into the dark as her eyes were still adjusting to the twilight.

"One second." He ducked down for a second. After he popped back up, he headed back for her, and it wasn't until he was a few feet away that she saw he had her bike.

"You didn't need to grab that."

"You forgot about it." He shrugged, lips curling up as he passed her and lifted it into the bed of his burgundy truck.

"You could have reminded me, and I would have grabbed it."

He wiped his hands together, turning to her and making a point to get close enough that she could feel the heat from his body, wafting toward her in the cool evening breeze. "Must you always be so independent?"

"*Must* I?" She mocked, and he cocked his brows as he grinned.

"I'll have you know, the English language is far too ample to not use it properly."

She narrowed her eyes at him, unaware of her smile, until he glanced down at her mouth. Her heart stopped for a second. Giving up trying to fight her, giving up in general before it roared back to life, thundering its beats unnaturally through her as she became hyper-aware of herself.

She tucked a strand of hair behind her ear, and he watched her the same way she'd resisted watching him. At least, he put on a t-shirt, though it only shifted her mind off his charm more than it was a real obstacle. Because even with his shirt on, he was just as alluring.

Her hand wandered to the door handle, and he unlocked it just as she did, almost sensing her desire to stop their tarrying glances. Had he wanted to end this connection? Had he given up on that date he had asked her on? Or was he simply just being a gentleman?

As she fastened her seatbelt, he started the car, and within moments, they were headed down the road, jostling about as they turned onto a cobblestone street. Though the day had been long and arduous, something obvious throughout it was the chemistry between them.

The silence in the car was a simmering pot, about to bubble over, and she sensed that now was the time to make her answer to him a firm one. She was determined to tell him no, to make it obvious that they could only have a working relationship and nothing more.

Her stomach twisted in an unexpected knot at the thought of saying that she wouldn't go on a date with him. Perhaps, her brain was completely fried from the sun beating down on her all day. That was the only explanation as to why she would have this small desire aching deep within. A flicker of what-if's all tied together with a ribbon and note that nudged her to say yes to him.

"What are you thinking about?" He tilted his chin in her direction, not breaking his eyes from the road.

"A lot." That wasn't a lie.

Caution should be given for moments like this. Something in the form of flashing neon signs, bold letters, and bright red lights.

"Lie, so you won't get hurt," one should say.

"Run far away, so your dreams don't die all over again," another would flash.

But all of them would ask her to stop in some way, shape, or form. That would have been ideal, perhaps even easier. Unfortunately, that's not how life worked, and it certainly wasn't how Sylvie's played out. Occasionally, it is the inevitables that catch us off guard—an ironic symptom of life.

With a heavy sigh, Sylvie looked up at the night sky, gaze wandering to the radiant North Star, seemingly shining brighter than all the rest. She had grown to believe something about it, how it always pointed her in the direction of her dreams to love people with everything she had.

A true north.

But when she was younger, she thought it would follow her. On long drives she would imagine that she and that star were friends, that she could trust every time she'd look up, it would be right there waiting for her. Following her every move to give her comfort at night.

It was during the cloudy nights that she realized, this

wasn't the truth. Sometimes, the night was simply dark, and there wasn't a shining beacon to ask her to keep going, or to show her the way. Yet, the sun would come up every morning, and that was a certain, definite, inevitable that she could always expect.

This was different, though—Ronan was different. She couldn't just expect him to be something she assumed. To say yes to their date would mean she had to get to know the real him. And maybe, that was scarier than imagining him to be this perfect, charming person with nothing but kindness in the warm heart beating behind his nicely defined muscles.

When the truck came to a stop in her driveway, she felt the pang in her chest. Everything tightened as he turned toward her.

"This is your stop." He jested, studying her face like it had a hidden treasure beneath its surface.

"Yes," she blurted, and he tilted his head, making her body feel flushed.

"So, are you going to get out, or...?"

"I mean, yes, I'll go on a date with you."

His smile dropped for the first time since she had met him, eyes wide and thoughtful.

Before he could say anything, she continued. "But, just this once. And only if you promise it will be private, that this would be kept a total secret. I'm not ready to explain myself to my sister and best friend, who are scarily close to seeing you drop me off."

He flicked off the headlight immediately, resting his

elbow on the center console for a moment to let her continue.

"That's it." She shrugged nervously, unsure if he would even want to go for it, considering her strict contingencies.

"Okay." He gave a quick nod.

"Okay?"

"Yes...should I put up more of a fight with you on it?"

"I just didn't expect you to say yes to me so quickly."

"Did you expect me to ask you what you're doing right now?"

"Sitting in a truck, talking to someone who just asked me a very obvious question."

"No." He shook his head, chuckling a hearty laugh that forced a smile on Sylvie's lips, though she was pretty sure he was laughing at her. "I mean, are you free right now?"

CHAPTER 6

Pine Blue Eyes

"Y ou want to go on our date right now?"

He looked around like it was the middle of the day and her question was nonsense before saying, "Yes, why not?"

She narrowed her eyes at him, unable to hide the grin tugging at her lips as she studied him. She should still back out, still say no, but nothing seemed as important as the look in his dreamy eyes or the way he leaned in, anticipating her response.

"I guess I'm going on a date with you, then." The words spilled out, so easily they scared her, especially since he turned the car back on instantly upon hearing them. They backed out quickly, headlights still off, until they reached the main road, and he whipped around, zooming down a trail she had never been down before. For miles, Country music played in the background as Ronan kept a sharp focus on the road.

They continued to curve small mountains and up

sloping hills. Dense tree-lines followed most of the road on either side, darkening the drive just a bit and hiding the starry sky above them.

After driving for a while longer in a surprisingly comfortable silence, Ronan brought the car to a stop at the edge of a thick forest. The high beams barely made their way through the density of it as he jumped out of the car and walked around to her side. She let him help her out, her heart a little jittery and uncertain of this date. She had already said yes, though. And they had driven all this way; she couldn't back out now.

His hand clung to hers, and chills spread steadily up her arm as they fumbled their way through the forest. They trudged up a small hill, and the sounds of rustling leaves through the wind grew louder. It reached such a volume that Sylvie eventually realized, it was not the wind at all but the sound of falling water.

As they broke through the trees and into a small clearing, there it was, the source roaring before them. She caught her breath as she marveled at the glorious waterfall, larger than she had ever seen, cascading down a mountain and into a pool of water that was so clear she could see little fish swimming under the bright moonlight.

"This is incredible, Ronan."

"I know."

They both took it in when she tilted her gaze up to him.

"Shall we?" He met her gaze as if he had sensed it

Her cheeks grew hot. "You want to swim?"

She looked back at the waterfall, thankful that the

space was dark enough for him to miss the redness of her cheeks, still beating with every blink.

"Yeah, don't you? After the day we had?" He chuckled, already taking off his shirt and running in the water with his shorts still on. Her jaw dropped at his lack of hesitancy, and her stomach churned at the idea of having to jump in the water without really knowing what was beneath the surface.

Perhaps, the clarity of the water was just an illusion, and it wasn't safe at all.

After dunking his head and swimming further toward the base of the waterfall, he turned his head in her direction, waving a dripping hand for her. "Come on! It's the perfect temperature."

She bit her lip before gritting her teeth. She could dip her toe in, test what he told her. Or, she could sprint forward, fully clothed, like a mad woman and join him. Her feet moved before she could choose the rational option, kicking off her sneakers and sprinting. Just as she leapt, a scream escaped her lips as the rush of falling overcame her, flipping her stomach as she plunged into the cold, clear pool.

It was deeper than she had thought, cooler, the farther down her body sank. She forced her arms and legs to shove her to the surface. Cool water waved through her hair and made her clothes float with her movements all the way to the top of the water. She reached for the moon, waving at her from just above the surface, and a hand reached down to meet hers, pulling her up and out into the air. She gasped deeply, head heavy with exhilaration like she'd never known, at least not for a long time.

"Are you okay?" Ronan searched her face as if there would be some indication of permanent damage, but the opposite was true. If anything, she'd come completely alive in a way that felt so irreversible, it was frightening.

"Yes." She breathed hard, and his brows pulled together.

"You sure?" She met his eyes when his voice was still heavy, and she nodded. His thick lashes were clumped together, blinking over his pine blue eyes with a concern she hadn't thought him capable of. He always seemed so carefree, but there was something that made her question where the root of that wistfulness came. It lasted only a moment because he was swimming away from her, splashing her playfully, before she could ask him what he was thinking.

She swam after him, tittering, until she reached his side at the base of the waterfall.

They played around, swam and teased like this for what felt like hours. The stars twinkled into the pool, rippling when they'd splash around like little kids. She felt young, younger than she remembered she could feel. The way he looked at her, their breathy laughs as they fought to see who could swim faster, made her heart pound with the rush of the waterfall pouring over them.

Eventually, their laughter carried them out of the water, and they laid in the lush grass that surrounded the waterfall.

"I haven't been here in many years," Ronan finally said after trying to catch his breath from their final race.

"*Years*?" She enunciated.

"Yeah." He shoved a hand through his wet hair, propping himself up on his elbow to look down at her.

"Why's that?"

He narrowed his eyes in thought. "It's complicated."

"I understand *complicated*." She laughed, more sarcastically than anything else.

"Oh yeah?" He laid back down next to her, turning his head to study her face. She felt his eyes wandering over her, waiting for a follow-up to her vague response. She traced the stars for a moment, staring intently at the way they gleaned and glowed.

"Yeah." Her heart skipped at the thought of sharing things she really hadn't spoken about with anyone.

"Three years ago," she swallowed the sick feeling in her throat. "I had a miscarriage."

She whispered the last word like it might hurt him the way it hurt her.

"I'm so sorry, Sylvie."

She shook her head, like it wasn't as heavy as it felt to carry.

"My husband at the time didn't want any more kids." She glanced over at him, noticing him studying her with such empathy that it made her more emotional. "We were already having so many problems to say the least..."

"You never have to say the least with me, Sylvia May." He interrupted in the brief pause she took to collect her thoughts. He added softly, "Just so you know."

Her brows lowered, eyes blinking a little more to compensate for the tears that threatened to spill.

No one had ever told her that before. Even her husband always used to order her to get to the point, to not tell stories so long, or recount every detail of her day. He wanted to have the briefest conversations possible, as if she was an inconvenience to him, especially toward the end. But Ronan wasn't like that. He seemed to enjoy her speaking and felt for her every word as if her burdens were his own.

"Communication became distant, cold. I think I resented him a bit, for stifling my dreams. He never wanted any of this for me, thought it was too impractical. He was a lawyer. You would think that would make for great debates, but really, it just caused us to drift apart. He threw himself into work, and when the kids left the house, I had enough of his cold shoulder."

Sylvie shifted her eyes to Ronan, who hung on her every word.

"I begged him to go to couples therapy with me, and he finally agreed. Then, I fell pregnant, and well, the distance was back. And it was like he couldn't stand to even look at me or sleep in the same bed. I only carried the baby for the first trimester, finally hopeful again that at least I could love and care for something. That at least I had a purpose. But when I miscarried..." Tears welled up in her eyes, and they streamed down despite her best efforts to hide them.

The back of his index finger was at her cheek, catching the tears before she could brush them away herself.

"It's a lot that's happened." She guffawed, as he retracted his hand, still listening. "For two years, we battled out the divorce. He got a penthouse in the Upper East Side, and I stayed in our home with my best friend, Meera. My sister and she were the ones who got me through this entire ordeal."

"That's why they came with you?"

"Sort of..." Sylvie tensed her brows, unsure if she should deliver the final explanation. "The day I arrived in Starwood, I had just come from the divorce hearing. They came with me, probably just to talk me out of being rash, but here we are doing just that."

She looked over at him, fully ready to see his face changing into an expression that would say 'nice knowing you, gotta go,' or something along those lines. But instead, he was smiling, his pink lips pressed together as he shook his head.

"You're a dreamer, Sylvia May."

"And unlucky dreamer." She rubbed her cheeks frustrated with the mix of emotions still swirling inside her. Her whole new journey had just began, and she had a whole lot of dream left to accomplish. Too many more obstacles in the way.

His eyes flicked between hers, sincere and unwavering. "Those who don't recognize your worth are the unlucky ones."

"Me? Lucky? Need I remind you that we met because I hit you with my bike?"

"But, out of anyone you could have hit, it was me—

owner of Ashton Housing. To me, that seems pretty lucky."

"Hm." She pouted her lips to the side. "I suppose."

"And it makes me lucky, too, because I am on a date with the most beautiful woman I've met in a very long time." He leaned in closer to her, his breath brushing against her upturned lips, causing her stomach to flutter.

"You're well-versed in flattery, Ronan."

"It's not flattery if it's the absolute truth." He arched a brow, tilting his chin.

"Is that how that works?" She bit her lip as he licked his, saying yes with the blink of his gorgeous eyes.

"Ronan?" She whispered, and his brows went tall with questions. "How did you get into your family business?"

"Besides nepotism?" He chuckled.

"Yes, besides nepotism."

"Well, my father's father started Ashton Housing, but my family has had ties to this land further back than that. I always wanted to be involved in the business, loved this area."

"It's a great area."

"It is. I started in construction. My father wanted to make sure I earned my place in the company. He was a big believer in never spoiling me. It was what my mother wanted before she passed. I was only ten, but she was my world, my father's, too. We were her moons, always clinging to her, wrapped around her orbit."

"How did she...?"

"Cancer." His eyes grew distant for a moment before

coming back to hers. "My father put me through construction, and I learned the ins and outs of actually building homes. I got to travel off the island and helped build countless homes in Massachusetts. It was a wonderful but atypical college experience. Then, when I came back home..."

That look in his eyes returned when he paused. They almost seemed to darken with an emotion she couldn't quite pinpoint.

"My father passed away a couple of years ago, so that's how I came to own Ashton Housing."

Sylvie couldn't help but notice how large of a time jump he had left in his story, but she didn't like that strange look in his eyes when he thought about it, so she left it be.

"Do you have any children?" She asked, and his grin grew in only the way a proud father's would.

"Yes. River. She's the best thing that's ever happened to me. Spirited, independent... And honestly, Sylvie, I think she's smarter than me most days."

They both laughed at this, a soft sweet connection of loving another human, raising them to become everything they'd ever hoped and more. "You have kids, too, I assume?"

"Yes. Four."

His eyes went so wide she could see more white in them than blue.

"Four?!" He exaggerated.

"Four." Humor imbued her tone. "Theo, June, Eleanor, and Ezra. The two youngest are miracle twins, but they couldn't be more opposite. Eleanor is so bright and soft-spoken, and Ezra is a wild card. I think he'd do anything if someone dared him. Theo is my eldest. Practical but brilliant and so creative. He's an artist. June is in love with cooking, and I think she'll be a famous chef one day. She's that good. She also has my first and only grandbaby so far, little Lucy."

"Lucy! That's adorable. I bet holidays are noisy and lively at your home."

"They were—are." She looked past him, almost picturing them crowded in the kitchen, all trying to do something to help but ending up making the entire process go that much slower. Her eyes snapped back to him as the image melted away into the recesses of her brain. "Favorite color?"

"Green." He responded with the same candor. "Yours?"

"Louis blue."

"That's quite specific." He chuckled. "What does Louis blue look like?"

"It's this pale blue that has more depth than a pastel, but it's still just as calming and pleasant to look at."

"Louis blue." His intent focus made it seem like her response was the most important thing for him to remember.

"Yep." She watched his expression change after taking it in.

"Favorite food?" He asked.

"Mmm, that's tough."

"I know."

"But, I'd have to say, pears."

"Pears, Sylvia May? *Pears*?"

Laughter started from deep within her gut and burst out of her, and he watched her with stars in his eyes as she closed hers to catch her breath.

"You can't tell me pears aren't absolutely amazing, Ronan," she finally managed to get out.

"I'm not saying they aren't. I'm just thinking if I had to eat them every day for the rest of my life, I might not feel so passionate about them. Not as passionate as you, anyway." His eyes crinkled at the corners as they maintained such intense eye contact that everything else around them disappeared.

"Fair enough." She wiped a tear, still filled with her joy, away from her eye.

"I'm gonna go with pizza."

"Pizza?"

"Yeah, for the rest of my life, I could eat pizza. You can put anything on a pizza."

"Even pears?"

"Gross." He grimaced, lips curling up at the edges. "But, yes. Even pears."

"Hm. Then, I'll change my answer."

"Oh?" He cocked his head, green grass pressing against the strong curvature of his cheek.

"My favorite food will be pizza, too."

"Woah, that's a big deal. You changed your favorite food for me. Does that make us official?"

"Ronan." She scolded, tapping his arm with the back of her hand as he snorted softly.

"Okay, okay. I've gotta take my shot when the

opportunity presents itself."

"Mhm." She sarcastically glanced at him from the corner of her eyes. Her cheeks hurt from smiling the entire night, so much so that she wondered just how long she had been talking to him, how often she had to catch her breath when she glanced his way.

"What time is it?" she whispered after they'd been looking into one another's eyes for longer than she would have cared to admit, especially considering this was only meant to be a one-time thing.

He lifted his wrist to check the time on his watch. Tapping it with his index finger, he pointed it toward the moonlight before looking back to her.

"It's 2:15."

"Oh my gosh, my sister is going to freak out." She sat up quickly, and he followed her, standing a bit quicker than her and holding out his hand to help her up. Their clothes had completely dried in the evening breeze, which made for a more tolerable trek back to the car. Her heart raced a little, fear permeating into her stomach at the thought of having to explain herself to Meera and Lyla.

When they made it to the car, she pulled her phone out of the cup holder, heart beating even faster as she turned it face up to her. Relief flashed through her when she saw that she hadn't received any calls or texts. At least, they hadn't even noticed her absence. Hopefully, they hadn't.

The drive home seemed even longer than before, but she continued to take steady breaths, trying not to worry about how much they had divulged to one another.

With each bend of the road, her body tensed, not wanting to move even an inch closer to him accidentally. This shouldn't continue. He was wonderful and new. But they were still in business together, and she couldn't risk something going wrong between them. She needed this bed and breakfast more than she needed the giddy feelings of potential love.

As they pulled into her driveway, her heart pounded steadily. He parked the car, lights already turned off so as not to flash them through the windows of her house. She turned to thank him because she owed him that. After the night they had, she felt as though she knew him better than she had ever known her ex-husband of twenty-nine years.

There was something there, a pull she couldn't deny but had to.

"Thank you," she whispered, and he leaned across to open her door for her. The scent of his hair was musky and intoxicating, sending heat flooding throughout her body and tension puddling between them as he slowly leaned away. His head hovered, stopping before getting too far from hers as she held her breath.

Those pine blue eyes glanced down at her lips then back up at her. His skin warmed the space between them, causing her lip to quiver, and her heart to react like a heavy, metal drum.

Then, before she could do anything else, frozen by the lingering attraction, and ensuing thumping of her longing heart, he inched in closer than before.

CHAPTER 7

Don't Turn Around

S ylvie cocked her head back, determined not to make the mistake of having his lips brush against hers. They were nearly there, about to kiss, her skin boiling from the heat of their connection.

"Goodnight," she whispered, and he pulled back, eyes still gleaming with the spark of desire that reflected the one inside of her.

"Hey." He caught her wrist as she turned to go, and she slowly turned her head, hesitant to hear the words forming on his perfect lips. "I'm gonna pick you up and drop you off every morning from now on, okay?"

She liked the way he expressed himself. Made it clear he didn't want her doing something that could harm her —or others for that matter. Yet, he still gave her a choice.

"Okay," she whispered back, biting her tongue a little too late.

"Goodnight, Sylvie May."

"Night, Ronan." She slipped out of the car and into

the early morning breeze that nearly swept her off her feet as she grabbed her bike from the back of Ronan's truck and pushed it to the door. She couldn't see his eyes clearly enough as he watched her quietly make her way inside. His tires rolled over the sand as it backed out of her driveway, and she slowly closed the door behind her, locking it immediately.

She didn't stop to catch her breath, but she felt as though she had run a mile. Instead, she hurried quietly up the stairs, avoiding the creaky portions of the steps and heading right for the bathroom. She wasn't going to go to bed in her dirty clothes, slightly stiff from having dried on her body in the salty air.

Her flowing blue silk nightgown was waiting for her on the counter with a towel, and she almost had a heart attack before remembering that Lyla was still in the habit of doing little things like that for her. After helping nurse her back to health upon having a miscarriage, she had done almost everything for her over the course of that entire year.

Sylvie sighed, touching the gown with her fingertips before rinsing herself off in the shower as quickly as she could. When she got out, she tied her hair in a bun and slipped on her nightgown before tip-toeing into her bedroom right across the hall. The breeze from the outside flowed through the windows as it did every night, and she was filled with a deep comfort as she curled into bed.

A few hours laters, her phone rang. Her eyelids flew open like she had only closed them just a moment ago to fall asleep. She rolled over, pressing the phone to her ear.

"Hello?"

"Good morning, Sylvia May."

"Ronan, why are you calling?" She swallowed to fix the dry patch in her throat.

"I'm here to pick you up. Are you still sleeping?" She sat up immediately, looking at the analog clock on her nightstand. In bold red letters, it read: *7:01 a.m.*

"I'll be right down," she blurted before hanging up and whipping the covers off herself. Her feet hit the wood floor with a thud as she ran into her closet and grabbed a pair of blue overalls and a white t-shirt. Quickly, she threw them on before nearly tumbling down the stairs.

"Good morning to you too, Sylvie!" Meera's voice was saturated with knowingness, but perhaps, it was just Sylvie's guilty conscience.

"I've gotta go! I'll see you later this evening?" Sylvie shoved her feet through her sneakers, grasping the wall as she looked over her shoulder to Meera, who was still in a robe.

"Okay, have a wonderful day." She took a relaxed sip of her coffee, and Sylvie felt a little relieved that maybe her initial inference could have been wrong.

"You, too!" she called as she grabbed her woven sun hat off the coat hanger and sprinted out the door. The sun was brighter than normal, more intent on making itself known. Her eyes stung as they adjusted, and she reached for the hot handle of Ronan's burgundy pick-up truck.

It met her hand before she could take a step closer, and she pulled it back the rest of the way as Ronan leaned back to his side of the car. She slid in with a heavy breath before closing the door behind her and buckling her seat belt.

"You get ready quick." Ronan glanced at the 7:06 a.m. on the radio clock. He was smug, probably because she had agreed to that date last night and definitely because he would be taking her to and from work every morning and evening. It was a recipe for disaster if she had hoped to keep her distance.

But that was the funny thing about waking up after very little sleep from the night with a very attractive stranger, who no longer seemed so strange. She wasn't sure if she wanted to keep her distance anymore. If their dates were anything like last nights, how could anything possibly go wrong?

Just before she was about to scold herself for not thinking properly before coffee, Ronan reached over with one in his hand.

"Dirty Chai, one shot of espresso." He beamed proudly as she looked at it in his steady hand. She couldn't help but wonder if he was a real person as she took it from him, mumbling a thank you that kept her hot cheeks from his line of sight. "There's an almond croissant in there, too. Elouise from the shop downtown, the Brown Bunny Bakery, she made these fresh this morning."

He pointed a finger to the crinkly white paper bag in the cup holder as they pulled out to the main road.

"You didn't have to do that, Ronan."

"I wanted to."

"I know... I just—"

"Just accept that I'm going to do nice things for you. And ask you on a second date."

Her stomach tied in a knot as she swallowed her drink, prepared to rationalize her way out of ever going out with him again.

"Ronan..." She stifled her instinctual response, but they were already at the site, and one of the construction guys tapped on Ronan's window.

"One sec." He waved a finger at the man and turned his entire body toward her. The man waved even more, knocking on the window with pleading eyes pointed right at Sylvie.

"It's really not a big deal, please answer him. He looks like he might combust." She looked past Ronan, who turned to see what she was talking about.

"Are you certain?" he asked over his shoulder.

"Yes. Please."

He rolled down the window and chatted with the man. It wasn't a long conversation, nor was it loud enough for her to make out every word. But when Ronan rolled the window back up and glanced at her with a smile so wide it could bridge the gap between continents, she knew something was about to happen.

"Looks like we need to go shopping."

"For the bed and breakfast?" she clarified.

"Yes. They're working with chemicals today, and we'd both need to sign waivers from the state to be on-site. So..."

"So, shopping."

"Yeah. You like interior design, right?"

"How did you know that?"

"I assumed." He was already shifting the gears to drive. She knew enough about the construction process that interior design wasn't their biggest hurdle at this stage of the build, but clearly it was all they were able to do today.

As they were pulling into town and parking, Sylvie asked, "Hey, don't you have work to do today?"

"What do you mean?"

"You know, don't you own a business?"

"Yeah, but you're missing the key word there...I *own* a business. I can do what I want, especially when it comes to work-related tasks."

"Ah, keyword *related*."

"I promise, you aren't taking any of my time up. This is a necessary run. I want to be here to show you the layout of the house. Then, you'll know what to get for it."

"Okay, but if you need to leave at any point—"

"I'll tell you, okay?"

"Okay."

They spent most of the day getting basic decor instead of trying to grab the major things, which would probably require them to take a ferry into the mainland. Most major furniture stores often didn't ship larger items to and from the mainland, especially not when customers could use their money to transport with ferries and shipping freights.

Meera and Lyla were especially probing at dinner, though Sylvie could tell by their questions, they had no idea just how involved she had been with Ronan the previous night.

"I think tomorrow, Ronan said we'd be checking the water lines and helping move in new wood for the build."

"That's a lot of manual labor," Lyla said, taking a bite of her wild rice.

"Well, I'm paying them far less than this place is worth, so it's the least I can do." Sylvie shot her a look as she took a sip of water.

"Ronan really gave you that good of a deal?" Meera leaned in, observing her reaction, which Sylvie attempted to keep as even as possible.

"He said the business will pay for itself one day and that bringing new people into town will only help him flourish."

"Hm." Meera nodded, and Lyla looked at her like she could see something radiating from Sylvie that no one else could.

That night, they watched another classic movie together, and Lyla was first to fall asleep. Meera dropped her head to Sylvie's shoulder as Lyla snored softly.

"Do you have any feelings for Ronan Ashton?" she whispered in the dark to Sylvie, whose stomach twisted with conflicted emotions not easily articulated.

"I don't know..." It was a half-truth but still a lie. Because even though she didn't know how deep they ran, she certainly knew they were there.

Meera's knowing smirk told Sylvie that she wouldn't let that answer fly for long, but she gained a reprieve for the night.

The next ·morning, Sylvie was already dressed in a white cotton romper, standing on the porch by the time

Ronan showed up in her driveway. As she climbed in the car, he greeted her with her favorite drink and a crumbly muffin that made her blink smiling eyes up at him. The day felt new, and even though she had toiled over her feelings for Ronan at night, when she was with him, it all felt simple. He was a breath of fresh air, the sunshine after a raging storm.

All those good feelings flew out the window the moment they arrived at the work site. Surrounding the bare bones of the bed and breakfast was Gertrude and a group of her townies, protesting with a megaphone and scribbly painted signs. Ronan parked the car, anger flooding his expression in a way that alarmed Sylvie.

"Stay here," he ordered, but she didn't listen, trailing behind him in the tall grass, right to the townspeople shouting nonsense about the build.

"It will dirty our water supply."

"It will pollute our air."

"We won't be able to leave the house without running into outsiders."

"We don't want this bed and breakfast. We don't want this break and breakfast." The shouts grew increasingly until Ronan stepped right up to Gertrude. Somehow, he had left her side; her feet had frozen her in place at the top of the hill.

Back and forth he went with her, shouts being carried away in the wind so that she couldn't hear a word. Then, he twisted around, red-faced, veins popping as he pulled out his phone, marching back up the hill to her side. She didn't say a word to him until he hung up.

"What are we gonna do?" She swallowed, and he turned his head to her, every trace of anger leaving his face. Concern replaced it. He must have seen her expression or sensed the waves of sickness crashing into her at the sight below them.

"It'll be okay. They'll leave." And he was right, they did leave, right after the cops escorted every last one of them off the premises.

Though they had left, and the workers began to get back to work, Sylvie still felt shaken by the entire event.

As her and Ronan went about the day, she couldn't break free from the worry welling up within her. She wanted her business to be successful, not the source of scandal and loathing from the very town it was planted in. And even though Ronan assured her that it wouldn't happen again, she was unable to figure out how he could be so sure of that.

"All right, boys. Let's call it," Ronan hollered as a round out thunder rumbled through the sky just a few minutes before the end of the workday. The group packed up, laying a tarp over the foundation as Sylvie and Ronan watched. She didn't realize that the entire time, she had been chewing on her nails, still worrying about Gertrude and her hoard of protestors.

"Hey." Ronan nudged her, but she kept her eyes fixed on the beginnings of her dreams, apprehension growing like the rain clouds in the sky. "You need to eat. You haven't all day."

"We've been working."

"It's no excuse. I should have gotten us food. Let me

make it up to you." His eyes were pools of purpose, pulling her in without her consent.

"What sort of thing were you thinking?"

"Huxley's Bistro in town is pretty remarkable."

"*In town?*"

"Yes." He shoved his hands in his pockets, his thick lashes blinking down at her. "Everyone will see us, and you know how I said we shouldn't make this a thing..."

"We won't. No one will see us, and we'll have a great meal. Trust me."

The problem was, she wanted to trust him. And despite how outlandish his claims were, she almost completely believed what he said was true.

"Okay." Her shoulders relaxed as he lifted his chin to the truck, and she followed him as heavy blots of rain began to drop. The downpour picked up just as she slid into the passenger's side, and Ronan started the truck. Her heart was jumping out of her chest as he turned them around and toward the town. It was disquieting, knowing that they were going into town together. And even more so because she had willingly agreed to it.

Had she lost her common sense when he batted his lashes? Or was it running into him just a week ago that had punctured her careful side and caused it to slowly leak out. If the latter were the case, she could only rely on the more frivolous parts of herself, like silly fleeting emotions for men too attractive to be considered safe. But he was—safe, completely and totally. That was how it seemed, anyway, and a part of her hoped he'd prove her wrong. That he would do something to help make sense of it all. Why would a man so kind and so genuine inside be wrapped in such an appealing package? How was he real?

As they approached town, he parked near a lamppost, directly across the cobblestone street from the restaurant he'd spoken of. It was bustling with people, another impossibility to conquer unless he wanted to eat in the car.

"Wait here, and I'll text you."

"You'll text me?" she asked, but he was already hopping out of the car with a wink.

"There's an umbrella under your seat." He flashed her a signature white-toothed grin before closing the door and jogging across the street.

After a few moments, her phone buzzed, and she clicked on his message.

"Sit in the third booth from the window, left side, tall candle in the center of the table."

She clutched her heart and whispered for it to shut up as she reached under the seat to grab the umbrella. After taking one last heavy breath, she opened the car door, and the whooshing sounds of a torrential downpour flooded her ears as she popped open the umbrella. Shoving herself forward, she crossed the sopping cobblestone, soaking her shoes in puddles with every step.

When she stepped up to the door, she shook out her umbrella, looking back at the car one last time before slipping in between an old couple and a young woman who had opened the door in her hesitation.

"Welcome to Huxley's Bistro!" A small teenager greeted her, his body language completely open and neutral for such a young kid.

She smiled back at him with a gentle nod as her eyes scanned the room for Ronan.

"Just one dining in?" He asked, and her eyes flicked back to him.

"Oh, uhm, can I sit over there?" She pointed to the empty booth where Ronan had instructed her to go.

"Wonderful, not a problem. Right this way, ma'am." He escorted her to the booth and sat a menu down in front of her. She was on autopilot when she ordered water with a side of lemon as the swirling questions led her gaze around the room.

Just before she reached for her phone, it buzzed in her pocket, and she pulled it out, reading the text on the screen from Ronan.

"Don't turn around."

CHAPTER 8

Blind Date

S ylvie immediately twisted toward the retardant bustling behind her just as a waiter brought water to the booth directly behind her, blocking her view.

"Thank you." Ronan's voice muffled from behind her, and the waiter waved a pleasantry before dashing off to another table.

"Ronan?" she whispered, and he chuckled just as her phone buzzed again.

"I said, don't turn around." It read.

"You're right behind me?" She sent it back.

"Yes. See, I told you I could make it work."

She shook her head, sitting her phone down just as her waiter came with her drink. As soon as he headed to another table, she craned her neck again.

"You're incorrigible."

"I'm seizing an opportunity, Sylvia May, not breaking the law."

"You didn't think we could sit in the car." There was a brief pause before her phone buzzed.

"That car wouldn't give you the full experience. Plus, Gertrude is notorious for reporting cars that have been parked in the main square for too long."

She could feel her lip curling; she grimaced before typing back. *"Good Lord, does that woman not have a life?"*

"She does, unfortunately." He whispered, and before she could ask what he meant, Sylvie's waiter came to the table.

"Ready to order?" He asked, eyes wide with genuine enthusiasm.

"Uhm..." She hadn't even looked at the menu.

Behind her, Ronan coughed. "Spaghetti and meatballs." He heaved between raspy breaths, and the waiter's eyes trailed to him skeptically then back to her.

"Oh, um, right. I forgot, I was going to order the spaghetti and meatballs."

The waiter blinked just a moment more before nodding his thick curly head of hair very slowly.

"All right, coming right up. Anything else?" he asked while looking at Ronan's booth, and her cheeks grew hot as she buried her head in the menu.

"That'll be it for now." She handed it back to him before he strode off.

"Nice going. Any other plans to make this more obvious?" she whispered, and he didn't answer. "Ronan?"

Worry accompanied her high tone as she began to worry that his coughing fit could have been real.

Her phone buzzed before she could peek her head into his booth.

"I ordered the same thing, so they should be out around the same time. You'll love it. All hand made, even the spaghetti. Nothing frozen except the veggies back there."

"How do you know this stuff?"

"I have my sources."

"Or secrets..." He reached his hand around and lightly touched her arm, shocking her and spreading chills over the space she touched. Her heart pounded heavier as he retracted it, and she touched the place he had with her other hand, as only to calm it down.

"I don't have that many secrets," he whispered, and she pressed her cheek to the red leather backing of the booth.

"So you do have some?"

"Doesn't everyone?"

"Tell me one of them." Her heart skipped as she waited for him to finally change her perception of him. If only he'd do something to make it easier to say no to him or divulge something too horrible for her to accept. The waiter brought both of their meals out on the same tray, grating fresh Parmesan over Sylvie's then Ronan's food.

"Would you like me to combine your tables?" He asked in a helpful tone.

"No," they quickly chorused, and the waiter glanced between them for a moment before lovering his chin.

"Enjoy your meal—meals." He twisted around, the grater under his arm, as he left their tables.

Her heart was thumping, but for some reason, even her shock of anxiety couldn't stop the small fits of laughter from spilling out. She tried to hold it in, but the more she suppressed it, the harder it fought back. Soon, Ronan was laughing, too, and now, they were alone at their respective tables, laughing like a pair of insane buffoons. Sylvie imagined mothers who would shield their eyes from the wild scene of cackling loners. Perhaps, skeptical townspeople would blame bad spaghetti for delusional fits, and they'd boycott the restaurant altogether.

But those were only erroneous thoughts that came in waves as she tried to calm herself down. The truth was a lot less funny, anyhow; Ronan and Sylvie could be spotted from any angle of the restaurant and despite their best efforts, people might still talk about their obvious exchanges. She pushed that thought away as they chatted and laughed with one another while enjoying their truly outstanding meal.

When it came time for the check, Ronan told the waiter he'd pick up the tab of the woman behind him and messaged her right as the man walked away to run his card.

"I'll meet you at the car."

She stood up and turned toward him. "Thank you for paying for my meal."

She nearly bowed to him, and he sucked in his lips to hide his laughter as she twirled around and made a bee-line for the door.

Outside, the rain had nearly stopped. It smelt like fresh dew and a hint of lemon. The cobblestone street looked as shiny as glass, reflecting every light still shimmering throughout the town. She walked across it, trying to avoid the major puddles, though her shoes were still soaked from the storm earlier.

When she reached the car, she slid in quickly, uncertain of who might be around and feeling a bit like a little kid hiding from a monster creeping around the corner. Gertrude did seem like a monster to her, though, even without knowing she could peer into Ronan's window at any moment and catch Sylvie sitting in the passenger's seat.

The rain began to pick up again but lighter than before, misting throughout the town and coating the car in droplets that eventually collected and ran down the glass.

Sylvie watched them for only a moment, wondering if the rain would slow things down for the construction the next day. Before she could grow too worrisome, Ronan hopped in the truck and turned the key in the ignition.

"Miss me?" he asked, patting the rain off his clothes.

Every anxiety vanished in his presence, and there was that peace he carried again, soft yet strong. She rolled her eyes sarcastically at him in response. She saw him reaching for her hand in her peripheral as they pulled out of town, but instead of fighting him, she met him halfway. When their fingers touched, she felt a spark that almost frightened her, but she let him engulf her hand with his warm, steady one. Everything about it felt right and equally scary. Not because it was forced but because the outcome of this touch was so unknown. This was sweet, absent of anything more than to show deep affection, like the connection they had, carving out new pathways for a life she hadn't even thought she wanted.

And perhaps, she wasn't ready, didn't want anything but her tried and true dream of owning that bed and breakfast, but this was something she couldn't put words to or envision when she closed her eyes. She was unable to dream up someone as perfect as Ronan Ashton.

The entire way home, he held her hand, and a rush of new and old feelings heightened her every sense. It tied her stomach into knots and flushed her cheeks with roses that wrapped around her rapidly beating heart.

"I can drop you off."

She shook her head vehemently.

"Please, Sylvia May, just this once, let me be a gentleman."

She quietly huffed to herself, glancing at the time and wondering if his presence in front of the door would cause a stir in the house. It was possible that the girls had already gone to bed or at least to their rooms. Regardless, he wasn't budging, and she had no real excuses left to muster, so she agreed.

Instantly, he took it upon himself to open her door for her, jumping out of the truck and crossing to her side.

"Thank you." She took his hand, still warm from their fingers interlacing the entire way home.

"My pleasure." He grinned in that crooked sort of way that only some people can pull off. Apparently, he was one of them. They walked to the porch and stopped in front of the door. Turning to each other in the dim porch light, his starry blue eyes danced between hers. "I had fun tonight."

"Me, too," she whispered back.

Somehow both of his hands were holding hers, fingers overlapping like a second instinct, and the silence between them brewed something much deeper than the surface where they bobbed.

"Goodnight," he said even softer, almost mouthing it as he blinked down at her lips. She watched his pout out just slightly as he brought his face even closer to hers. Her heart raced, skin pulled toward him like she was tumbling through the wash cycle, stuck to him, though she wanted to pull away.

Just before their eager lips touched, she turned her head toward the door, and he gently kissed her cheek. Every affection from his lips spilled across her skin like ink on a page, and she wanted to truly touch her lips to his, but she couldn't. And he must have sensed this because he stepped back, letting go of her hands as he offered a sympathetic smile and headed back to his truck.

In a daze, she turned around, unlocking the door and creeping inside, her heart slowly sinking from the heights it had been rising to only moments ago.

She blew it, giving away that she was a mess to be avoided, not a love interest to be pursued.

Yet, he stuck around. And each week, he asked her on another date, more intimate and special than the last.

The following weeks were filled with those types of moments: stargazing in his pick-up truck, painting at an empty beach in the early morning, meals in neighboring towns where they pretended to be visitors from further down south.

As the house progressed, so did their relationship. Eventually, Sylvie could not remember a time when they weren't sneaking around with one another, when he wasn't in every minuscule and dominant moment of her life. Everything had progressed so quickly, and she wasn't sure how long it was sustainable before everyone found them out. The world was moving at one pace while she was circling it with Ronan, and it didn't seem appropriate to hide. She had still not told her counselor, sister, best friend, or children.

It seemed like an impossible feat to do so. She was already in so deep with him.

It was August, late Saturday afternoon, and Sylvie sat on the porch swing as she looked at the color-changing trees dancing in the wind when her phone rang in her lap.

"Hello?" She answered before looking.

"Hi, Mom." Her eldest son chirped. "I just finished those flyers, and I'll send them out to the rest of the family to post as soon as you approve them."

"Wow! Theo, that was so quick. I just asked you yesterday. I hope I didn't interrupt your workweek."

"Not at all. It's pretty easy here, too easy." He mumbled the last part, but she heard him.

"I thought you liked being a magazine cover designer?"

"It's honestly too much to get into right now, Mom."

"I'm sorry. I didn't mean to push."

"No, you didn't. It's just—it's a sore spot is all."

"Okay." She felt a lump in her throat, the one that often came when she took on her children's problems as her own.

"But hey, would you take a look at those flyers? I sent them to your email."

"Yes. Let me look right now..." She fiddled around, trying to figure out where the heck her email app was. Her technology skills were embarrassingly non-existent. But she was only embarrassed by it around her kids, who had grown up their entire lives with technology. "All right..." She stalled until she finally tapped hard enough on the screen that somehow it brought her where she had wanted to go.

After accessing his email attachment, she saw the beautiful design. It was a grand opening flyer with the gorgeous finish outside the bed and breakfast. He had digitally gone in and photoshopped it based on Ronan's drawings. Underneath the home, among the tall wispy grass, was a sign on the white picket fence with the details for the grand opening of the bed and breakfast.

"Theo, it's gorgeous," she breathed.

"You think so? I'm so glad you like it."

"Yes, I do. Thank you so much, sweetie."

"No problem. I'm glad I could help, even though I can't break away from work to be there. All of us kids will post on our social media about it and keep our fingers crossed for you."

"You're a remarkable son. You know that?"

"Thanks, Mom. I gotta go."

"Okay, love you."

"Love you, too." She waited until he hung up and laid the phone down beside her, inhaling deeply before resting her head back against the swing. She looked over the horizon where the North Star gleaned even before the sun had fully set.

"Long week?" Meera's gentle voice asked as she stepped outside with two cups of spicy hot chocolate. It didn't feel like fall yet, but Meera insisted on doing all of her fall traditions. Her children wouldn't make it down for the grand opening of the bed and breakfast either, but she still wanted to bring all the memories of the seasons changing to their little rental home by the beach.

"The longest." Sylvie chuffed and scooted over for Meera to join her. Steadily, her bare feet brushed over the white wood deck until she sat next to Sylvie, handing her a mug.

"Thanks." Sylvie took it as Meera gently nodded, her large caramel eyes blinking peacefully.

"So, how's construction been? I heard they're nearly done with the inside?"

"Yep, light fixtures are going in on Monday."

"What about those doorknobs you chose?"

Sylvie chuckled, remembering the look on Ronan's face when she had said she'd like to have different door knobs on every door. "They're already in the doors, which I decided to have painted in different designs when we get a little more money. So, each room has a personality."

"You're brilliant." Meera grinned into her mug.

"I couldn't have done this without you, Meera."

"What about me?" Lyla wrapped her fuzzy robe around her as she hobbled out of the house dramatically.

"Oh, of course, that's a given." Sylvie corrected herself

just as Lyla sat down on the other side of her. "I couldn't have done this without either of you."

She took their hands in hers, looking between the two of them, trying to reveal from the depth of her core how utterly blessed she was to be loved and supported by them, but no two words could do that justice.

"Thank you."

"You're worth it." Lyla rested her head on Sylvie's shoulder.

"I'd do the same for both of you in a heartbeat, no questions asked. You know that, right?" She looked to Meera, who pulled her hand up to her mouth and kissed it gently.

"We both know you would, sweetheart."

And the evening air felt a little cooler than the nights before, as if this conversation was the blessing the weather needed to fully change into fall. Perhaps, this was the moment that Sylvie needed, to remember that blessings weren't always as tangible as words exchanged between loved ones, like the moment she was in. Oftentimes, they were actions amounting to something much more lasting and impressionable. Something you could feel, rather than hear, see rather than touch. Something like the love between family, chosen and blood.

Though Sylvie knew their love for one another would never change, guilt still churned in the pit of her stomach about sneaking around with Ronan. There was a part of her that maybe still believed there was reason to be cautious, though they were moving at lightning speed.

There was still something, a wall, or a secret he was

withholding. And she had many examples of times that made her weary of it, but before she could explore the thought any deeper, she was drawn from it by the buzzing of her phone. As if thinking about him had caused him to think about her, too, his name showed on her phone screen as an incoming call.

"Are you gonna get that?" Meera asked, looking down at about the same time Lyla did. Sylvie panicked, jumping up so quickly that she knocked her hot chocolate from between her legs onto the porch.

"It's work." She shrugged, jogging inside and up the stairs, closing the door behind her and getting as far away from it as possible before answering.

"Hey," she whispered.

"Hey," he whispered back, and she rolled her eyes, but couldn't keep the smile from her lips that always seemed to be present when Ronan was speaking to her. "Tonight, I want to take you out."

"Where?" She didn't even question it anymore, didn't put up a fight. He knew as well as she did that whatever they were was inevitable. Risky, but inevitable.

"You'll have to just see. I'll pick you up in half an hour."

"You have to give me a bit more warning next time you have something planned. Now, I have to pretend to turn in early."

"Or, you could just tell them about us..."

"*Or*, no, thank you. You have me for a few hours, and then I have to go to sleep because tomorrow is a very big day."

"All right, all right. I'm honored to have just a morsel of your time."

"Yeah, yeah." She giggled. She never giggled before knowing him. It felt almost silly, but he made it make sense.

"See you soon, Sylvia May."

She tossed the phone on her bed, taking a long breath before quickly changing into a Louis blue cotton dress with puffy sleeves, a fitted a-line and sweeping tea length skirt. She let her salt-kissed waves go where they may, collecting just the top half of her hair and braiding it out of her face. After one last look at herself, she stuck her head out of her room, glancing down the dark hall.

"I'm turning in for the night." She called down, and there was a brief pause before Lyla answered.

"Is everything okay?"

"Yeah, yes. I'm just so tired." She forced a fake yawn that she hoped sounded real. "I'll see you both bright and early in the morning."

"Okay..." Meera sounded hesitant, but they both chorused their goodnights. She waited at the door for it to grow silent in the home, watching the time carefully.

When it had been twenty-five minutes later, Sylvie slipped into the hallway that was dark and silent. She patted across the grooves of the white wood floor brushing beneath her bare feet, as she made her way to the staircase. It was pitch-black downstairs, which either meant the girls had put on a movie or they had gone straight to sleep.

She couldn't be too cautious though, so as she stepped down the stairs she held her breath, using careful light movements so as not to draw any attention to herself. She could go out the back door, so she wouldn't pass the lounge room if she saw them watching a movie, and she bent over to peek into the lounge. It was as dark as the rest of the first floor, though, so she continued down further and stopped.

The clustering sound of metal beads knocking their way through an opening alerted her before the lamp even turned on. She was a frozen deer in headlights, and the headlights were her sister and Meera. They stared at her with such shock that it almost reflected her own as she looked back at them, mouth slightly parted.

"What on earth are you doing?" Lyla's hands were already on her hips as Meera glanced out the window, eyes going even rounder when she no doubt saw the burgundy truck in the driveway.

Sylvie's shoulders dropped, like the weight of bearing such a secret had become all too much, and as if her lips were no longer connected to her body, she sighed. "I was going on a date with Ronan Ashton."

CHAPTER 9
Cracks

"Ronan Ashton?" Lyla stepped forward, shaking her head in immediate disapproval. This was the conversation Sylvie had wanted to avoid. The one that reminded her of the very real realities of dating someone she was working with, right after getting divorced.

Then, there were Ronan's walls. He never seemed to fully open up, specifically about his family; she noticed it when she asked questions. Knew he had a daughter, but he rarely spoke about her. Though their relationship was on some sort of fast track, and they were learning so much, he still hid so much from her.

Everything about them seemed to fit, but that's what scared her. It was too perfect. So, maybe she was imagining this barrier, and all the secrets shielded from her on the other side of it. Tonight, she thought she might bring up her concerns, but by the look in her sister and best friend's eyes, she could no longer keep her secret from them.

"Yes." She hung her head, sitting down on the staircase as they joined her on the steps below.

"How long has this been going on?" Meera asked.

"And why?" Lyla blinked angrily.

Sylvie understood why they would be cross with her, or hurt. They had given up months to be with her through so many hard times; going through depression after a miscarriage, working through hrt two-year divorce, and then choosing to go with her on a crazy adventure to Nantucket. It wasn't exactly a great way to repay them by gambling her dreams for the first attractive man to show interest in her.

So, she told them everything, all the ways she felt about him and the apprehensions, and even about how they had started these frequent, secret excursions. They listened intently, though Lyla's unshifting anger remained present in the creases of her face, her lips ironed straight.

"Do you know how hard we have worked to care for you and ensure you have this dream you never even told us you wanted until six months ago? We didn't come here so you could play at falling in love, like some teenager and derail it. We came here hoping that you'd figure everything out. It seemed like you had, but now... Now, I can't understand why you would want to invest any time in something that botch the success of the business you're about to open." She shook her red face before taking another breath, finger wagging in the air.

"I think what Lyla is trying to get at here is a lot deeper than she's conveying," Meera said softly, before Lyla could continue to rebuke Sylvie. "Our concern is about how quickly you've moved, considering how recent your divorce was. That's not a judgment call at all. I just think I'd like to know more about him if I was in your shoes."

Sylvie took a breath to speak, and maybe to fight back, but Lyla said, "Where is his daughter's mother? How does she fit into the picture?"

"I—I don't know. He doesn't like to talk about that..." Sylvie winced.

"Doesn't like to or won't?" Meera's brows turned up in an expression that gave away just how concerned she was for Sylvie.

"How old is his daughter? Does she live with him or the mother?"

Sylvie grit her teeth, unable to answer because there was no answer. She knew very little about those things because he kept them to himself. Pushing seemed to rock the boat too much, and the truth was that she was having too much fun with him to really dig into his psyche for answers that might ruin everything.

It was too late to hide her feelings about their questions, though, because they kept barreling through, spit firing back and forth like shots without warning until she could no longer take it.

"Where does he live?"

"How did his father pass away at such a young age?"

"What are his motivations for your relationship if you don't even spend time around other people when you're together?"

"Does he turn away from you when he's on his phone?"

"Enough, both of you!" Sylvie nearly shouted. "I know all of this. Don't you think I've toiled over it in secret? I'm not daft. I was just finally feeling the freedom of being single. For two years, I struggled with an endless divorce and the constant loneliness longer than that, shackled to the old ways of my life falling apart around me. But for the first time in so many years, I've met someone who seems to fit me so perfectly it hurts to think about it ending. So, I avoided the signs that told me to ask him more questions, push harder when he grew quiet, tell him I needed an answer or I would end it. I didn't have the strength. All right? Is that what you wanted to hear?"

She held back a soft sob before burying her face in her hands. "I'm weak." She whimpered, and Meera placed a hand on her knee.

"You're one of the strongest women I know. Your family deserves better than for you to bring a man with seemingly more issues than your ex into the picture. You deserve better than that. After everything you've been through, you should focus on what really brings the light to your eyes and the joy to your heart that I haven't seen in so long—your bed and breakfast."

Sylvie knew the voice of reason she had been lacking was no longer just knocking at her door but sitting in her living room, giving her an order to listen or lose everything she'd worked for. Somehow, keeping Ronan to herself would only bring her more pain, and she knew it without a doubt as the ones closest to her pleaded for her to see what had been right in front of her all along.

"It's better to end it now, than to end it over a blow-up

fight. Animosity will only cause things to spiral. If you end it like a mature adult, a part of you you've clearly been neglecting, then everything can continue the way it needs to for the grand opening of your bed and breakfast." Lyla raised her brows that almost said more than her harsh words.

"Yes, you should refocus your energy on what really matters," Meera added, with a softer edge than Lyla's.

Sylvie's hope waned as they spoke, falling until it had disappeared into a despondent pit. She really couldn't afford to ignore their caution or their disapproval. They knew her best, and she owed them for everything they had done to help her get to where she was now.

"What would I even say to him?" She forced her lip not to quiver, though her voice still shook a bit.

Lyla stood as she answered. "Something logical. You know him better than us. Tell him what will make it quick and painless."

Quick and painless? She wasn't so sure how that could be synonymous with the type of relationship her and Ronan had built. Though she was uncertain of the secrets he was so clearly hiding, she trusted him enough not to pry. And there was an understanding between them that made everything work. They fit, so pulling apart would hurt more than she cared to admit, but it had to be done.

Her legs were already moving down the stairs, bare feet tripping over themselves as she stumbled to the door. With one last look at the girls, she swiftly made her way out the door, heart pounding in her throat as she stepped off the porch and right to the truck. Her door opened wide when she got close enough, and Ronan's kind voice greeted her.

"Going barefoot tonight, Sylvia May?" Her name on his lips sounded especially heartbreaking.

"Ronan..."

"You might need some shoes where we're going, if it's not too much trouble to go back inside and grab them." Either he wasn't reading her tone, or he didn't want to. And she thought him too smart to be that oblivious.

"You've been helping me so much with this bed and breakfast, and I'm so eternally grateful that you have..."

"But?" His brows pulled together as he leaned toward her, concern filling his every feature and making her feel even worse than before.

"It's just, you'll be so busy with new customers after tomorrow, and I'll have a business to run..." Why couldn't she just say it?

"We'll have time for each other. I promise you that," he blurted, and she only shook her head in response.

"I think both of us knew this couldn't go as far as we wanted it to. I think this is it for us."

"You're breaking up with me?" he softly asked as she turned to her bleary eyes from his, looking at the porch light, promising her company after she shattered her own heart. She nodded, unable to form the words after a small squeak escaped her tightening throat.

"I don't understand. I thought we wanted the same things."

"It's just—"

"I thought you were being guided by that North Star."

He pointed up to the sky, but tears made it impossible to see anything up there. "I thought that your dreams to love and be loved were up there, guiding you to this place, guiding you to me."

That shot an arrow through her heart, and the first rogue tear spilled out onto her cheek.

"Sylvia May, I love—"

"*Don't say that,*" she said, a little angry now that he was willing to risk everything to make her stay, when she was willing to risk everything to leave him. He cocked his head back, alerted by her tone as she repeated it in a shaky whisper. "Don't say that, please. Especially not when you're withholding so much from me."

"What do you mean?"

"If you can answer this, I'll go out with you tonight." She didn't want to give him an ultimatum, but there was still a part of her that didn't want to give up just yet.

"Anything," he pressed.

"Where is River's mother?" It was the only thing she could think to ask because it was the most poignant of all the questions zipping through her thoughts like shards of glass. He paused, a strange look overcoming his face and slumping his shoulders in a way that she could not understand or fully recognize. His eyes went distant and for a moment.

Maybe, just maybe he will save us with his well-kept secrets.

But after shifting his jaw, he turned his face toward her, glowering before softening his eyes, defeated.

"I won't hold you back from living the life you've

always dreamed of, even if it's without me, Sylvie." Her name, being said the way that he never did, was a proverbial break between them. The snapping of the strings holding them together like a mystical force of destiny.

But he wasn't her destiny; he couldn't be. She had to accomplish her dreams. Love could wait, if that's what this was. So, she backed up, wiping a tear from her cheek that was instantly replaced with another.

"Goodnight," she strained to say.

"Goodnight," he whispered back as she gently closed the door and watched him back out of the driveway for the very last time. It was most certainly not a *good night*.

She choked out soft sobs, watching his truck stir up dust in the dark driveway before it hit the road and zoomed off. Just as her knees began to quiver, arms were around her. Lyla and Meera steadied her in the quiet of the night; only her sobs were audible. Not even the wind that so often blew through the town could be felt. Everything was still, somber.

Eventually, they coaxed her inside, brought her to the couch and plopped a bowl of homemade vanilla ice cream on her lap with a heaping scoop of her favorite hot fudge from the ice cream shop just up the road. Lyla chose a cheesy rom-com. It had some title she didn't recognize with overly attractive actors, considering their main personality trait was meant to be ugly nerds.

Most of the evening her eyes were wet with tears, despite her best efforts, and when she went to bed that night, all she could think of was the moment he drove away. Why did it feel like he had taken her dreams in the bed of his truck and carried them from her? Her dreams were about to come true. Tomorrow was the grand opening of her bed and breakfast. That should have been a source of excitement, but her stomach was filled with dread, even as she closed her eyes and forced sleep to come.

In the morning, she rolled out of bed, eyes still half-closed as she fumbled through her things in the closet. She chose a cream, colorfully embroidered mid-maxi dress with frilly sleeves that she had found in a thrift store on the south end of Nantucket. As she slipped it on, she pulled her waves back into a low updo, with pieces falling around her face that she had enough time to curl. After covering her exposed skin with sunscreen and patting on some rose blush and lipstick, she headed downstairs. Meera was in the kitchen, preparing breakfast still. When she saw the silkie, she looked at the clock on the wall in shock, then back to her.

"You're up earlier than you need to be."

"Couldn't sleep."

"Well, I wouldn't have been able to tell. You look gorgeous, Sylvie."

"Thank you, Meera." She sat at the bar, watching Meera make French toast with her famous chicken and corn scrambled eggs. It was a hard thing to explain to anyone else, but it was absolutely incredible. No gooey egg texture to them, what-so-ever. And just enough spice that they seemed to be perfectly curated for the fall.

Even the fragrance in the kitchen made her warmer inside, like a small slice of hope was beginning to rebuild itself in her shattered heart. Somehow, even with fragments, her heart was still beating, and she had to keep going despite the pain. Ronan was just a stepping stone on her journey. That's what she told herself.

The sooner she believed that, the better because she would have a business to run. Hopefully, a busy one.

After Meera had served her breakfast, Sylvie realized there was a very vital piece missing from the table.

"Where's Lyla?" She asked after shoveling a bite of unbelievable food into her mouth.

"Oh, she had to run into town this morning to grab a few things before the opening. She'll meet us in time for the grand opening."

Sylvie looked through the front window as Meera spoke. "Why is her car still in the driveway then?"

"Oh, I dropped her off. She'll take an Uber to the bed and breakfast."

Sylvie bobbed her head, sensing something was a bit off, but she didn't have much capacity to investigate it, so she finished her eggs.

"Oh, speaking of the bed and breakfast, have you landed on a name just yet?"

"No." Sylvie shrugged, hoping she would have already come up with something by now. Even though it was a longstanding dream, she hadn't ever wanted to name the imaginary bed and breakfast. That might make it too real, too heartbreaking.

"Well, I'm sure you'll figure something out before we cut that blue ribbon." She gently cupped Sylvie's hand.

"Yes." Sylvie forced a smile that surprisingly felt

genuine when she truly thought about the reality of that bed and breakfast awaiting her. "Me, too."

After the both of them had finished breakfast and Meera had changed into a beautiful sage sari dress with gold embellishment, they headed out the door. The morning fall air felt crisp and fresh, setting the tone for the rest of the day. Sylvie soon forgot everything else that was troubling her as the anticipation of seeing her fully finished bed and breakfast grew within her.

The drive was quiet but quicker than Sylvie expected, and before long, they were sitting right in front of the home.

It was everything Sylvie could have ever dreamt up and then some. She got out of the car in a daze, her heart bursting from her chest as she stared at it in awe.

A white picket fence surrounded the home, along with beautiful blackberry bushes and white flowery ones she had never seen before. The slate, gainsboro, and taupe cobblestone led to the white wood wraparound porch. For Hanna's swings, seating areas and gorgeous bright green plants covered vacant spots and hung from the ceiling where wide-blade fans slowly turned.

The beautiful wood paneling of the house was Louis blue, spanning every inch that wasn't a white balcony with flowers cascading off them. It was three stories high with a Cape Cod style black roof, except for the spiral part of the roof at the far-right edge with acutely placed, stained glass windows.

She took a shaky step forward, noticing the glass greenhouse just to the left of the home, with little stepping stones leading to it. As she reached the blue ribbon, set up to be cut, she saw the stunning front entrance. They were towering double doors, dark blue painted wood, with a large dome window on each side.

The air smelt clean and sweet, like cotton, but spicy and warm like cozy autumn only comparable to a fall-scented candle with woody undertones.

"Oh my gosh," she whispered under her breath as Meera reached her side.

"This is all yours," Meera said gleefully, disbelief ringing through the air like wind chimes.

A car door shut behind them, but Sylvie barely made note of it until all-too familiar arms were wrapping around her, snuggly. She twisted around in them, utterly gobsmacked.

CHAPTER 10

An Unexpected Guest

"June?" Sylvie looked down at her daughter, beaming up at her proudly, bright blue eyes glistening with fervor.

"Hi, Mom!" Her melodic voice rang.

"What are you doing here?" Lyla bounced over, Lucy, on her hip.

"Grandma!" Lucy squealed gleefully, reaching for her.

"I thought I'd come to help make a menu and lead your kitchen team for a little. That's assuming you need the help?" She shook a hand through her bleach-blonde pixie cut sheepishly.

"Yes! That would be incredible! But what about your job at the bakery, honey?" June pulled away, waving a delicate hand dismissively.

"Eh, not to worry. I've decided to go on an extended leave. I still want to open my own bakery one day. So, this experience will help me as much as it will help you."

"You are all things wonderful, June Jasmine Atwood. Have I told you that?"

June laughed as Sylvie pulled her into another tight hug, and Lucy ran over to join in, her strawberry curls bouncing with her tiny feet. As the little girl collided with Sylvie's leg, she pulled Lucy up on her hip, and the three began discussing plans as a few cars arrived at the property.

Within the hour, there was an inconceivable turnout, and the townspeople of not only Starwood, but surrounding towns, had come to support her. After spending all she had left and even borrowing some to make this dream a reality, the reassurance from everyone felt well-worth it. It was the first hurdle to jump before she could attract real customers. And perhaps, some of those customers were in the crowd, having seen her flyers and being interested in the quaint beauty of this tiny town.

She took a shaky breath as she stood on the porch and looked out at the townspeople, gearing up to step toward the ribbon with her closest people by her side. But just as she turned, a loud crack broke out in the center of the crowd, causing people to part from it as Gertrude Price was lifted into the air with a megaphone in hand. A group surrounded her, chanting incoherently as she yelled over them in a grainy voice filled with hate.

"We won't be silenced. We won't be pushed out of our home. We don't want this bed and breakfast in our town."

Meera leaned in, shielding her mouth from the crowd as she whispered in Sylvie's ear, "No one is giving her any points for that chant."

Sylvie shook her head, wanting to laugh but not feeling very cheery.

She was dampening the entire event, making the guests feel unwelcome, and other townspeople left questioning what side to be on.

Maybe that wasn't the case, potentially everyone was just as fed up with Gertrude as she was, but it didn't make it any easier to endure.

Just before it could get too out of hand, she saw a figure barreling toward the group. It knocked the tower of people supporting Gertrude down to the ground just as a few police men joined the man in guiding the entire group into cop cars.

"Now, I can't practice my right to freedom of speech?" Gertrude shouted as they closed her in the car, a familiar figure slipping back into the crowd that she recognized as Ronan. So, he had helped her even after their unfortunate end. This stirred confusion within her, twisting her stomach and reeling her mind.

Her best friend and sister were right about him, even if this meant he was truly a good man. He was just a distraction, one that could never be fully trusted because he kept his cards so close to his chest.

The mayor stepped up the front porch steps with a pair of large gold scissors. He bowed his nearly bald head to her as he handed them over.

"Thank you for your courage to bring new life to our town. It is not only needed but wanted. You're wanted here, Ms. Blythe. Everyone who has shown up today believes in you."

It could have been his words or the fact that she tangibly felt the crowd's support, but tears welled up in her eyes as she stepped to the microphone in front of the blue ribbon. The crowd instantly fell silent as she tapped her finger on it, causing a thump then brief ringing before she nervously brought her mouth to it.

"People of Starwood and beyond, I'm so grateful for your love and support. This bed and breakfast has meant everything to me, even before its conception. I'm here to tell you that whatever you dream, you can do. You make anything happen, if you work hard, believe in yourself, and accept help from those around you."

She looked back at her family, chosen and blood, joined with smiles on their faces and hearts extended to her.

"I want to thank all of my loved ones for helping me reach the stars when I thought I was only capable of being planted on the ground. And," She turned back toward the crowd. "I would like to thank each one of you for making this possible and spreading the word further than we could alone."

The crowd cheered victoriously, and she felt as though she was about to charge into battle with everyone behind her. They were there to support this place. And though there had been opposition, she felt nothing but their reassurance.

"That being said, I want to dedicate North Star Bed And Breakfast to the dreamers. To the ones who let their passions and pursuits drive them to achieving their wildest, most outrageous ambitions. To you, I say, thank you and never stop dreaming. The world needs your light."

The crowd exploded into cheers and excitement, buzzing straight through the air like an electric current. It was palpable, and knocked every nerve out of her as she stepped up to the blue ribbon. She waved a hand to her family behind her, and the girls joined her sides.

"Together," she ordered them all with a grin and held on to her as she cut the ribbon.

Her heart soared in a way she never thought it would as the people clapped along with the music blaring through the speakers. A song she hadn't heard playing over their excitement as she pulled her family into a hug. This was a moment she hadn't even gotten to think about because of the whirlwind her and Ronan had been engulfed in. But today was about her, and all the people who helped her get to this point.

That made her think about how she wished to hug him, thank him for every string he had pulled to make this possible, but she couldn't even bring herself to search for him in the crowd. It was too late for them, so hopefully he knew how much his efforts had meant to her. Without them, she might still be searching the town for someone to believe in her dreams as much as she had all of those stifling years.

But as she looked over her families, proud faces and the crowd's sheer excitement, she felt the reassurance of each one of them. With love like this, how could she not succeed?

~

It had been weeks since the grand opening of North Star B&B. Just as Sylvie predicted, business was going incredibly well. The support of the surrounding towns, and everyone from the mainland, had gained her a spot in some of the most distributed newspapers in the eastern parts of the US.

Lyla headed back home just after the ceremony to be with her family. After a teary goodbye and many *thank-yous* that could never amount to the sacrifices she had made for Sylvie, they parted ways.

Meera had delivered that news that she would be staying to help with the marketing side of the business, since her degree in college had been for just that. She was also superb with the written word, having published parenting books under a pen name. Sylvie was so grateful for her help, but also her company after completely cutting herself off from Ronan.

"Sylvie!" Meera whispered harshly, shaking her awake in the early winter morning.

"What?" She groggily whispered, eyes still glued together as she unsuccessfully fought Meera's hands.

"As of today, December 1st, we are officially listed on Airbnb and guests that have already stayed with us are leaving five-star reviews."

Sylvie's eyes flew open and were met with a bright laptop screen as she sat up. She skimmed through some wonderful comments from guests that she immediately remembered upon seeing their names. All of them were incredible and even more meaningful to her seeing just how deeply they felt her love.

"I have one more really exciting piece of information."

"Okay?" Sylvie blinked, unsure of why Meera always had to build dramatic tension, especially when she knew how deeply Sylvie felt everything.

"It's probably one of the best things I could tell you this morning, first thing, bright and early—"

"Okay, Meera, out with it!" She laughed with a roll of her sleepy eyes.

"All right. There are a ton of comments that talk about the menu and how unbelievable it is. People love June's cooking."

"That's great!"

"But that's not the best part. With so many impressive reviews already, we have enough people booked out for the next couple of weeks. With my trend predictor, I can confidently say that there is a very likely chance that business will be steady from here on out."

"Oh my God, Meera, this is incredible!"

"And!" She wagged a finger for Sylvie to wait for even more information that she couldn't possibly figure would be bigger than the already remarkable news. "We can hire June full-time, permanently."

"Really?" Sylvie gasped, so amazed and excited to deliver the news to her daughter.

"Yes." She grinned so wide it made everything seem possible.

Is nothing ever going to be impossible from now on? She slid out of bed and sprinted down the stairs, intending to go right to the kitchen to tell June the good news. As she twisted around the last set of steps, and left to the foyer, there was a knock at the door. Through the glass, she saw the figures, and without thinking, she darted to the door, opening it up before remembering she was in her pajamas.

"Good morning." The familiar candor of a voice she'd forgotten she enjoyed reached her ears before her eyes caught up with what was happening.

Ronan Ashton stood tall in a business suit and long charcoal jacket, his hand on the shoulder of a girl, not much younger than her youngest daughter, Eleanor.

"Good morning," she forced out, trying not to inspect the girl too hard.

"This is River, my daughter," he said and River pushed her long copper waves off her shoulder.

"Nice to meet you, River."

"Likewise, Ms. Blythe." She reached out a freckled hand, and Sylvie took it with a kind smile that took some effort to muster in lieu of her shock.

"What brings you both here today?"

"Well, River here has been begging me to come and visit. She has a passion for cooking and has heard of Chef June's skills. I was sort of hoping she'd be able to shadow her for a while, just to see if this is what she really wants in a career. Maybe learn a thing or two." He was nervous. She could tell, but the curl of his lips and the heat from his breath that formed clouds around his face.

She wanted to say no, she did. But she had yet to thank him properly for all he had done for her. And that weighed on her for weeks on end, every time she avoided him in town. So, without showing as much reluctance as she felt inside, she gently nodded.

"If it's all right with June, it's more than alright with me."

River grinned a bright smile that reminded her of Ronan's as she leapt forward, embracing Sylvie in a tight hug.

"Thank you, Ms. Blythe," she practically shouted.

"Of course, I'll take you to her now."

Ronan mouthed a thank you, and Sylvie blinked back, hoping he could see she meant to tell him the same.

She shut the door and ushered River to the kitchen around the corner. The sights and smells of everything cooking and moving at once were already traveling down the hall. As they entered the kitchen, swiftly passing through the double doors, June was instructing one of the chefs on the way she wanted the special bread she'd added to the menu.

"June!" Sylvie waved, breaking her out of her focus. For a moment, her eyes darted with alarm, and then she snapped out of it, softly grinning before striding to them.

"Morning! Who's this?" June got straight to the point, always had since she was very young.

"This is River. She was looking to possibly shadow you. She's thinking about being a chef one day."

"All right." June grabbed her pointed chin, nodding to herself for a moment. "Okay, yeah. That works. Ash, off the bread. We've got a newcomer who's gonna work on it!"

Resting her hands on her hips, she gave River another once over.

"Grab an apron and meet me over there." She pointed to the metal table in the center of the kitchen, and River hopped right to it, no questions asked.

"Thank you, June." Sylvie squeezed June's arm affectionately.

"It's no problem, Mom." She was about to head off, but Sylvie kept her hold.

"Yes?" She leaned in to Sylvie.

"The role of head chef will now be paid full-time, permanently." Sylvie beamed as she announced the news to her daughter, who immediately pulled her into a hug.

"Are you serious? This is incredible news!"

Sylvie held her daughter close, as long as she would let her.

"All right, I have to get back to it." June pulled away, with one last look of excitement, before bobbing over to River.

Sylvie clutched her chest as she walked out the door, ready to announce breakfast to the guests waiting in the front room lounge by the fireplace.

Every day was sunny and bright, though it was winter, Sylvie felt the warmth of love as it poured out of her and onto her guests. Whatever they needed, she wanted to provide. And the more guests she cared for, the greater number of reviews they received on their property.

Weeks went by and though much continued to change, one thing remained the same. Every morning, right before the day had truly begun, Ronan would drop River off on his way to work. He and Sylvie would awkwardly stare at one another, forcing pleasantries and faking smiles, though there was barely an exchange between them. But every time she saw him, her stomach knotted in that way only he could make it, and her heart raced irrationally fast.

River was a delight to have around, and customers loved her, so Sylvie decided to consult Meera, about hiring her on part-time.

"It will be great because June says that River paused working toward a degree in food science for this. We can offer her part-time if she promises to go back to school at the start of the year," Sylvie assured Meera, who was doing an extensive search of the financial records as they spoke.

"Hm." She lowered her reading glasses to the tip of her nose as she searched over the papers before pulling them off and setting everything down on her desk. "All right, I like it. People really do love her."

"She's got a great, bubbly personality," Sylvie agreed, heading down the steps to welcome River with the wonderful news. She hadn't looked out the window yet, but if she had, she would have seen the mounds of snow, piling up and whipping through the air in flurries.

After passing the stall window on the main staircase, she stopped, panning her head across the white covered world outside. Her guests would need extra logs, warm ciders and hot chocolate available all day for the inconvenience of being snowed in.

No one was going out in this weather, at least not until they sent snow plows from the mainland, which could take all day. Ronan hadn't called yet; that was very odd, and a pit formed in Sylvie's stomach as she paced by the door for a moment more, hoping they'd show and something horrible hadn't happened.

After a while of pacing, she decided to go busy herself elsewhere, but just as she stepped up the first stair, the doorbell rang. She whipped around and leapt to it, pulling it open and immediately regretting her haste when the most bitter air blew through the door, stinging her eyes and skin.

She stepped back to shelf herself with the door, and River burst in, wearing a heavy jacket and far too many layers that were oversized to be hers. Sylvie stuck her head out the door again to see Ronan's beet-red skin, wet clothes, and caked snow all over his flimsy button up olive slacks.

He was on the brink of freezing to death.

CHAPTER 11
That's How They Fell

S ylvie acted upon complete instinct.

"Come inside." She grabbed Ronan's frozen arm as he rigidly moved indoors and ordered, "To the fireplace."

River held the other side of her father as they ushered him into one of the front rooms with a large fireplace against the wall.

They sat him down in a blue velvet chair, and Sylvie left them immediately, too panicked to say anything. She sprinted up to one of the guest rooms that was vacant, but the last guest had left some warmer clothes in the closet. She grabbed the thick knit turtle-neck without a second though and some thicker black slacks before sprinting back down the steps.

It was good that no one was awake yet because this would cause quite a stir that she wasn't wanting her bed and breakfast to be known for. Her socks slid across the wood floors as she stepped back into the front room where

River had laid his coat back over him. He was rattling through his own personal earthquake, and his lips were turning slightly blue.

River's eyes were tearful as she knelt beside him. There was no doubt this was bad, but Sylvie couldn't think about the horrifying possibilities of this situation worsening, so she laid the clothes on the chair beside, taking a shaky breath.

"Ronan, can you change into these?" she asked, trying to keep her voice as calm as possible.

"Y-yes," he forced out through clicking teeth.

"Okay, we'll give you a minute." She grabbed River's arm without thinking and pulled her into the hallway.

"Wait, I want to make sure he's okay."

"He'll be fine, River. I promise." Sylvie closed the door, not sure if she even believed her words as she struggled to stand. River was beginning to shake with the shock of sobs ringing through her small frame.

"Hey, hey," Sylvie whispered, taking her shoulders in her hands. "It's going to be okay. Just go down to the kitchen and get some peppermint tea from June. You can get to work as one of the waiters brings it out to us. Okay?"

"But, I want to make sure he's okay."

"He will be fine. If anything changes on that front, I will run to you immediately."

Her teary eyes clung to the closed door, longing brimming her desperate expression.

"All right," she croaked before rushing to the kitchen.

After a few minutes, Sylvie pressed her ear to the door, unsure if she should knock just yet.

"Tea, ma'am?" She jumped back, craning her head around. One of the men from the kitchen stood two feet away, holding a tray with a teapot and mugs.

"I'll take it in. Thank you." She took it, and he darted away as she held the tray with one hand and knocked with the other.

"Come in." Ronan's warm voice relieved her some as she opened the door, stepping inside. It was warmer since the door had been closed, trapping in the heat. He turned his head to her, offering a soft stubbly grin before looking back to the fireplace as she sat in the seat next to his.

"Tea?" She asked, setting the tray on the glass coffee table.

"Yes, please." His eyes were on her as she poured him a mug, placing it in his ready hands. Thankfully, his lips were back to normal, but his skin was still pink in places as if he had gotten a sunburn.

"What were you thinking? You should have stayed home today."

"I had to meet an important client, and the snow didn't look so bad. Not until we were in it."

"What happened after you hit the road?"

"Everything was fine until we were about a ten-minute walk from you. My truck broke down. Gave out. I guess it was too cold." He shrugged, taking another sip. Sylvie watched him, studying the fire before his sharp eyes met hers. His perfect pink lips curled the way they always did,

MOLLY SUMMERS

evoking a sense of home in a place she had already thought couldn't feel more so.

"That truck is ancient." She huffed a laugh before taking a sip, and his hearty one bellowed as he shook his head.

"Yeah... River has been begging me to get rid of it for the longest time."

"You might have to know."

He labored a breath, that spark of joy leaving his face, making Sylvie remember why they couldn't be any more than this in the first place.

"Yeah." He finally nodded, and she thought that was all he'd say.

"But," he continued, and her heart fluttered. "I have to teach River to drive, so it's gotta be something easy for her."

"So, she doesn't know how to drive?"

"Nope. Can you believe that? Twenty-three years old, and she refuses so much as to get behind the wheel. Mostly, she bikes, but I won't let her bike this far out. You're on the edge of town, and it's a lot for her to do every day and night."

"Not very safe either."

"Yeah. Exactly."

"So, why?"

"Why what?" His brows tensed sincerely.

"Why doesn't she drive?"

He tilted his head for a moment before shaking it, lips pressed flat. "She has her reasons, I suppose."

"Hm." Sylvie didn't know whether this was a wall or

him opening up in his own way. She wanted to believe it was the latter, but she wanted to avoid getting her hopes too high. The moment of impact after the fall would only hurt so much worse.

"And you?" He turned his head completely to her.

"*I*, what?"

"You have your reasons, too."

She stared at him blankly, hoping he could see she was not connecting the dots. "... For?"

"For ending things with us."

Her heart immediately fell to the floor with a thud. Of course, she had her reasons. She made some of them pretty clear and others rather vague. But she couldn't very well hope to share them when everything inside of her broke at telling him they were over. It's not as if she had a speech planned for him. Everything had happened so quickly.

"Yes." She forced her gaze on the fire, crackling in the smooth stone fireplace.

"Can I ask you a question?"

She sensed his gaze on her in her peripherals. "Sure."

"Why is it that the bravest woman I know would be so scared to hold on to a good thing?" Involuntarily, her head tilted to him. His eyes searched her, unapologetically.

"There's not enough time for us to talk about this right now."

"Sylvia May, there has never been another woman like you. You're radiant. Even when I don't want to think about you, I do. I hate the way you make me feel when I'm near you. I have tried to let it go, but I can't."

"Ronan."

133

"Please, just listen." He paused, waiting for her to nod once before continuing. "We could never work if I forced this on you. I just know there is something special, different, good, between us. I don't regret what we had, and I won't regret asking you, begging you, to at least give me a second chance to prove myself worthy of someone as incredible as you."

She held her breath, sitting her mug down on the coffee table as she tried to remain calm. She could give him a million excuses as to why they shouldn't go there again, but nothing seemed to be as important as this intangible connection between them. It was what the moon was for the tides, what kept the earth from sinking into itself.

"I can give you time to think about my offer. I just want you to be happy." His voice was soft as he tried to maintain eye contact, but she couldn't look at him. She knew his gaze would only weaken her crumbling stance.

Though there was much reason to be hesitant, his promise seemed to cover every base. And the longer they sat in comfortable silence, the more her heart beat in a familiar pattern. One that had been forgotten since being separated from him. She would be lying to herself if she were to say that she hadn't deeply regretted breaking up with him. But she had found many things that vied for her attention, outside of her broken heart, and those things repaired some damage.

There was still a gap though, a space left for him that she almost felt aching as he spoke to her of his feelings. She felt them, too, knew them too well to be okay with just ignoring them.

"You and River are welcome to board for free tonight until the snow plows are sent through the main roads. I've got one extra room upstairs," she offered after the tea had grown cold.

"Thank you. That's very kind. And I mean it about taking your time to think about what I said. You're worth waiting for." He weakly pressed his lips together

It was unfair how he could say things like that to her, and her body betrayed her resolve with its desires. She stood, walking to the door. Just before she stopped to open it, she couldn't keep herself from the instinct deep within that told her not to go. Sylvie turned around on the impulse, shocked by his frame trailing close behind her.

"Oh," she breathed, and the knot in his throat moved up then down as he took a step back. "I was just going to say that...well, I don't really know how to say it."

His brows turned up at the corners, pine blue's searching like speed-reading the pages of her thoughts.

"I don't need time to think about this."

"Oh..." he breathed despondently.

"I want to make this work. But without sneaking around. I'm ready to be with you for real."

His eyes lit up brighter than the fire behind him, a grin reaching his cheeks and creasing his face in the most endearing way.

"Well then..." He beamed. "In two days' time, we'll have a date at Lombardi's."

"The Italian restaurant in Brighton Town?"

"Yep, the very one!" And opened the door for her, letting her walk ahead of him. Though it was in the town over, and they had been there before, it was a nice idea, thinking about them walking in together, hand-in-hand. It was their favorite restaurant, so she knew that's why he wanted to take her there instead of somewhere in their town.

She felt ready, excited about the possibility of finally starting fresh. There was a small fear, still adamant about not letting her forget it.

It clung to her subconscious and danced around her impulsive whims. There was no doubt, still, walls that Ronan Ashton hid parts of himself behind. But if his promise were true, then perhaps, she'd find everything out soon enough.

A few more weeks went by, and nothing slowed down, not even over Christmas as they had thought. By the new year, Ronan's business was booming, and so was North Star Bed and Breakfast. There was a constant need for great lengths of effort to balance their relationship with the ever-increasing work.

Meera had been relatively calm when Sylvie broke the news of her and Ronan.

"That man has secrets. Be careful this time. Don't get too invested without knowing everything," Meera said.

All had been well, but she couldn't help but feel that their relationship was the same as it had been. Late night dates in different towns, early morning activities before the sun had risen, and long calls on the phone after everyone had gone to bed.

Somehow, they felt exclusive and not just in a commitment stance, but in a social stance, too. Separated from everything but each other when they spent time together.

One night, Meera had come into her room with some milk and cookies, which meant she wanted to talk.

"So, how has it been with Ronan?" she asked, cozying up on the bed.

"It's been good. It's been hard to keep up with everything. Our businesses are both really taking off."

"Is that worrisome?"

"No, no. I actually love the hustle, and so does he. I wouldn't want to complain about it to him. He's been trying hard to make it work. We both have. Plus, I love the way he makes me feel. He's kinda the perfect guy."

"*Perfect*?"

"Yes... Why'd you say it like that?"

"Well, shun me if I'm out of line here." She raised her palms in surrender. "But has he opened up to you about the things he seemed to be holding back?"

Her question irritated Sylvie, but she knew it was only because Meera was right. Ronan hadn't opened up about those things and seemed to evade them just the same as before. But she blamed it on him being tired from work or having other things on his mind. Though she knew she was just prolonging the inevitable conversation. The one that would blow up in her face if she didn't carefully word it. Even then, it was highly flammable, and her prodding would be just a lit match.

"I'm not ready to ask him anything he doesn't willingly tell me."

"That's basically the diplomatic answer for *'yes, he's still being weird about things.'*" Meera raised her brows as she dunked her cookie into the glass of milk between them, and Sylvie shoved out a heavy breath.

"Okay, I get it, Meera. But it's not what makes or breaks our relationship, not at this point anyway. I thought you were supportive of us now."

"I am, but I'm mostly supportive of *you*. He's just a man that might not always be around, but you're my best friend." She gently placed her hand over Sylvie's. "I want you to be happy and fulfilled."

Sylvie tilted her head, a sympathetic smile leaking through. "I am. Really, I promise."

That answer seemed to cap that topic, and they moved on to other things, laughing as they normally did about random guest interactions or funny moments throughout their day. Though they didn't speak of her relationship with Ronan for the rest of the night, the things Meera said to her had stuck.

Sylvie cared too much about her friends and family to ever blend someone into their lives that was not meant to be there. But Ronan was incredible, even when he wasn't with her, he'd send her flowers or write her a note.

The weight of their relationship was held equally between them. She never felt as though she was giving too much, and he too little. It was the most balanced she had felt in any relationship, and there was no doubt they shared a passion as much as an attention to the details. He paid mind to what mattered. Often, that was small things, the things that no one else would know or think of unless they truly knew her heart. And he did, very well.,

Nevertheless, to overlook the things that concerned her, deep down, would be wrong. So, perhaps a conversation was needed to make everything right, to smooth it all out and make plain what needed to be shared for her to feel at ease.

As she curled up in bed that night, her thoughts were all on Ronan. Everything they had ever experienced, right from their happenstance meeting. Were they aligned like the stars? Or accidentally bumping into each other on the way to something greater for them both? She wanted to believe that they were destined, but the mysteries he kept only pushed her to feel the opposite.

A sick feeling curled in the very depths of her uneasy stomach as she went to bed. Something more tangible than the soft flannel sheets she was engulfed in glided to the forefront of her mind. It was a lingering question, one she feared held great consequence, should it be revealed. *What is Ronan Ashton hiding?*

When her alarm sounded in the morning, she didn't get out of bed. For the first time in months, perhaps years, she snoozed her alarm, turning over on her side to look out her towering windows. The snow that had fallen weeks ago lingered in patches around muddied grass and naked trees, bending beneath the wind's howling attempts to pass through unobstructed.

It reminded her more of New York, more than it ever had in Starwood. But it didn't feel like the place she had wandered from almost a year ago. It felt like home, comfort, and family. She knew, no matter the outcome of her conversation with Ronan, that would never go away. It hadn't in his absence, and it wouldn't again if he refused to tell her the truths he hid from her.

With a deep stretch that made its way to her stiff bones, she rolled out of bed with a nod and sunk her feet deep into a thick, fluffy pair of slippers. Grabbing her burgundy robe off the seat at the end of her bed, she slipped it on and headed out the door. They had made it fairly warm throughout the bed and breakfast in the evenings to ensure that no one would be shivering like that first fall of snow a month ago. So, the warm central heat blew through the air as she stepped down the staircase, passing each level with quiet caution so as not to prematurely wake any of the guests.

When she reached the main foyer, she made her way to the kitchen, where only a few cooks had begun prepping for breakfast. They buzzed around, jazz music softly playing in the background as June carried Lucy on her hip, testing out some colorful breakfast tarts on the counter.

Sylvie watched them together and couldn't help but feel proud of the mother her daughter had become. Left to be a single parent in a city that was unforgiving to people who could not afford it, made her way into one of the most prestigious cooking schools and eventually a world-renowned bakery. It was enough to make her teary-eyed. June turned around just in time to see her eyes glisten with the fervor in a way only a mother's could, and she smiled softly to say hello.

Sylvie nodded back, watching her work for a moment more before grabbing a coffee from the pot that had been freshly brewed and heading back out to the foyer to wait for River's drop-off. It might not have been the best time to speak with Ronan about everything, but it had to happen. She had to know what he was withholding, no matter the outcome of her asking.

The doorbell rang as she was beginning to pace, and everything stood still for a moment as her feet thudded across the wood floor to the front doors. She made a conscious effort to breathe deeply, sighing through a clenched jaw that puffed her cheeks as she unlocked the doors. Slowly, she pulled them open, so as not to get blasted with cool air, but River did not immediately step inside like she normally did.

Sylvie stepped into the doorway to see what was going on, and her heart stopped, lips parted, eyes blinked rapidly to decipher what she was actually seeing before her.

There, on the front porch of her bed and breakfast, was Gertrude Price, hands on both of River's shoulders as she pursed her lips, narrowing her eyes at Sylvie.

"Well, don't just stand there, welcome us in." She scowled in a nasty sort of way that made Sylvie more cross than she already was at the sight of her.

"Um, I don't think you're familiar with how this works, but usually if you're escorted off a premise, not once but *twice*, you're not really welcomed back at that establishment."

She cocked her head rather abruptly for someone so old and stiff. "I should hope I will be welcomed inside my *granddaughter's* work."

"*Grand*—" Sylvie shook her head, thinking perhaps she had heard her entirely wrong. "I'm sorry, I'm lost. How do you know Ronan?"

Her sparse brows went so tall they nearly got lost in her silver Edwardian Pompadour hairstyle. "My, at the very least, you're somewhat pretty."

"Excuse me?" Sylvie barely got out.

"I'm Ronan's mother-in-law."

CHAPTER 12

The Scorned Woman

T he instant the words fell out, Sylvie's brain forged connections that she could not deny, nor could she show how greatly they distressed her.

"Well, thank you for dropping her off, Gertrude." Sylvie plastered on a smile that made her chest ache as River stepped inside and made a bee-line for the kitchen.

"Good day." Gertrude's lips pursed into a smile as she sauntered off the porch and back to her car. Sylvie closed the door and leaned against it, attempting to catch her breath. Though she stood still, her heart raced faster and faster, causing her head to spin and her vision to blur.

"Sylvie?" Meera's soothing voice called from somewhere, and then arms were around her before she could wave to show where she was. Meera was her life vest, carrying her back to shore. They entered the front room, and she closed the door before her. Sylvie tried to focus on the towering dark sage bookshelves, observing every wall and rising to the towering wood ceiling with an eclectic chandelier. She tried to count the specs of light it split and spread throughout the room and down the towering window on the front wall.

"Sylvie, look at me." Meera crouched down in front of her as she endeavored to remake calm, though everything felt very broken and confusing inside. "Sylvie, what happened? Do I need to call a doctor?"

Sylvie forced her gaze to Meera's caramel pools of concern, wide and searching.

"I'm okay," Sylvie whispered, unsure how to make everything pull apart the way it had connected in her brain.

"You don't seem okay."

"I am." She swallowed the truth like a large pill without any water to wash it down.

"Tell me what happened." Meera insisted, grabbing Sylvie's hands in both of hers.

"Gertrude." She felt her eyes toggling as the memory replayed.

"She came here?"

"Yes."

Meer's lip curled up at one of the corners as her brows lowered. "What did she want?"

"She dropped River off."

"Why?"

"Because...she's Ronan's mother-in-law."

"Ma...*mother-in-law*? You don't think..."

"That Ronan's married, and that's why he's been so secretive, and completely fine with our relationship always being kept under wraps? Yeah."

"Sylvie…" Meera breathed, eyes filling with tears that Sylvie couldn't yet muster. Shock riddled through her body, and nothing was processing just right. Every moment they were together, and he shied away from questions about his family, the way he only spoke about River and never had anything to say about her mother, even the times that he called her late at night. Had he done all of this behind his wife's back?

There was no other explanation that would reveal a different truth. Gertrude made it clear who she was. And though the woman was stuck in her ways and loudmouthed, she wasn't a liar. Not to Sylvie's knowledge. River didn't debate it or say anything about it either that would have made Sylvie believe this to be some sort of elaborate scheme.

Why would she scheme anyway? It's not like the town knew she and Ronan were dating. How could they when they were so hidden from the world around them?

"You should at least talk to him? I mean, Gertrude Price isn't exactly reliable. Is she?"

"I don't know. Seemed pretty legit to me."

"Well, I think you should talk to him before you jump to any conclusions."

"I'm not jumping to conclusions."

"I can see it in your eyes that you are, Sylvie."

"I'll call him, okay?"

"All right. You want me to stay with you while you do?"

"Yes, please." Meera squeezed her hands reassuringly

before letting go, and Sylvie pulled her phone out of the inside pocket of her robe.

Quickly, she clicked on his name in her call history, and it rang a few times before going to voicemail. She cocked her head in disbelief, looking at the screen.

"He sent me to voicemail." She uttered before clicking his name again. Meera took a breath to speak but appeared to decide otherwise as she watched Sylvie bring the phone to her ear again. It rang a few more times than the last and clicked over to voicemail again before she received a text from him.

"I'm in a meeting. I'll call you when I'm out."

Sylvie read it then showed the message to Meera who squinted at it in annoyance.

"I'm going down there." Sylvie stood up, crossing to the door.

"Going down where? To his work? Sylvie…" Meera caught up to her, stopping her from opening the door by shoving her palm against it.

"What?" Sylvie snapped, not about to let anyone break her the way she had been broken for far too long.

"You should wait to talk to him before doing anything rash."

"You are the one who told me just last night that I should talk to him."

"Not like this." She shook her head. "You know I didn't mean it like this."

"Well, how could you have? You didn't know I was his side piece."

"You don't know that either."

"Not yet." Sylvie pushed Meera's hand away and whipped over the door, running through the foyer and grabbing her keys off the key hook.

"Sylvie!" Meera shouted after her as she sprinted down the front steps and to the car they shared.

"I'll be back!" Sylvie called, jumping into the car and forcing her eyes away from Meera's because she knew what her face would look like. She knew she was acting crazy, but that's what Ronan had made her.

She was no longer waiting on anyone to get answers, she would come at it head on. That seemed to be the only way to resolve the issue, now seemingly far worse than she had initially anticipated.

She sped down the road and through the streets of town, her mind racing along with her heart, as she tried to take deep breaths. Every star was aligning, dots connecting, but not in a way that gave her any hope of them working out. By the time she haphazardly parked in front of his work, she was convinced what they'd had was nothing more than a tawdry affair all along.

Not much could change that, and the reality of it was like standing in the center of a forest fire. She was burning as she jumped out of the car and marched up the stairs to his office building.

"Good morning." The receptionist dully greeted her, not at all sensing her pure rage until Sylvie said nothing to her, barring past her and to the glass door that led to the main office.

"Ma'am, you can't go in there without an appointment," the receptionist called after her, but she

147

continued marching, searching the desks and meeting rooms until she spotted Ronan with a large group of men at a long wooden table. She sped up, headed right for them and not stopping for anyone who asked her what they could help her with.

She thought she must have looked crazy, still in her pajamas and slippers, hair a wavy mess and eyes burning holes in anyone who smiled her way. But nothing would stop her as she swept past her reflection in the glass walls, to the door of the conference room.

Her hand was on the doorknob before she could catch even the faintest semblance of common sense, and she shoved it open, hoping it shook every wall in that room.

All heads turned toward her, even Ronan's. His eyes grew wide with concern as she stepped closer to him, fighting the urge to yell in his face and accuse him of being a two-timer. Instead, she took a sharp inhale before continuing.

"Ronan Ashton, are you cheating on your wife to be with me?"

All smiles and snickers ceased. His concern fell flat, lips pressed together as he turned back to his colleagues.

"I apologize for this. Just one moment." He approached her, and she placed her hands on her hips, knowing full-well her face was probably a red shade that only happened when she was in a hysteric rage. Her heart beat in her eyes as he pinched the space between his brows.

He looked up once more, his expression unreadable. "Please leave."

His response was a slap in the face, so cold it made her

shiver and her eyes water because the realization that she had been right was enough to make her fall apart like paper in water. If he had nothing more to say to her than this, then she was done. She had to be, for her sanity and for the ethics of such a complicated relationship.

But her feet were stuck to the floor, she couldn't move, and maybe he saw it. Saw her on the brink of combusting. How silly she had been to think that she was going to be the match to light the explosion. Turns out, he had been holding a flame under her all along.

"I'll explain everything later, Sylvia May," he finally said, a strange shift in his tone as she shook her head at his words. This was not the answer she needed because she was no longer in need of him to confirm anything for her. He had answered her enough.

"Ronan Ashton, I never want to see your face again. Don't call me, don't come back to the bed and breakfast, and most definitely, do not ever call me Sylvia May again!" She screamed the last part, had to get it out of her lungs so that it'd stop puncturing holes in her heart and spreading the sickness of betrayal through her shocked system.

Ronan stared at her, either dumbfounded or completely crushed. She hoped it was both—that he couldn't bear the sight of her leaving as she turned on her heel and marched out the door. No one stopped her or said goodbye on her way out. If they had, she couldn't hear them with the ringing in her ears, like right after an explosion. In a way, she had just stood in Ronan's office, a grenade in her hand, but he had done nothing to remove it before it ignited.

As she started the car, tears poured from her eyes, dropping to her lap as she turned down the narrow cobblestone road and back to the bed and breakfast. Clouds had started to blow in from the east as a wind picked up that warned her of the storm about to fall on them. She didn't know if she could take another wintery blast, an icy cold prison that would lock her in the house for God knows how long.

Still, she kept her hands steady on the wheel, void of energy to fight the sobs shaking her core as she pulled back into the driveway of the bed and breakfast. Everyone would be finishing up breakfast by the time of her arrival, so she sat in the car to calm her shaking nerves, blot her splotchy cheeks, and dry her bleary eyes. It was a task that she knew how to do because it's something all mothers were so familiar with. That was a strength of hers—hiding emotions to make sure everyone else was okay.

After a few more moments of deep breaths, a thick snowflake fell onto the center of her windshield, and she shook her head, knowing she was about to brace the cold once more. With a labored sigh, she stepped onto the frozen grass with her slippers. The air was even more frigid than it was when she had left earlier, and she crunched over the ground, wrapping herself in her robe as tightly as she could. Millions of fat snowflakes fluttered around her, endlessly dropping to the ground and promising a day inside for the entire household.

They would have to offer baking classes with June and perhaps even bring down the extra board games that no one had played yet.

It was remarkable how ignoring her crushed heart allowed her to reel through the to-do lists of her mind. She tried not to think about that fact too intently because it would ultimately lead her back down the trail of replaying today's events all over again until she was in hysterics.

She shivered as she reached the door, the exposed skin burning from the freezing temperatures as she jammed the key in the keyhole. Before she could turn it, the lock clicked, and Meera whipped open the door, pulling her inside.

"What happened? Is everything okay?"

"Yes, we have a lot to do. Another snow storm is coming. I need all the events and activity options for today laid out on a pretty list and posted on everyone's door within the hour."

"I think you should sit down for a second, Sylvie. We should talk about what happened? Did you see Ronan just now?"

His name brought fresh hot tears to Sylvie's eyes, but she turned toward the dining room and blinked them away. "We could set up games over on that table, maybe an art class with Ally, our gardener who does those murals in town. Then we can—"

"Sylvie, stop." Meera grabbed her shoulder, and the second she did caused every emotion to surface. She had forgotten that faking it never worked with Meera. She saw everything, even the hidden turmoil Sylvie tried desperately to bury. All it took was for her to turn back to Meera, and her entire body caved in on itself, legs finally giving in as she sank to the floor.

Meera followed like a mirror, pulling her into the warmth of her sunshine embrace. But not even her kind rays could break through the icy storm leaking from the newest breaks in her permanently damaged heart.

"Oh, Sylvie. I'm so sorry," Meera whispered, brushing the lengths of her hair from the crown of her head in long, comforting strokes.

"I shouldn't have ignored all the signs." She sobbed in a way that made her feel like she was talking underwater.

"You love so deeply, Sylvie. It's your greatest strength and, perhaps, your greatest weakness all in one."

Sylvie let the tears overtake her, her body giving in to the depths of her hardest realizations waving through her like the aftershock of an earthquake. She knew she couldn't indulge in this much longer, knew the guests would need someone to care for them and give them a wonderful experience, even though the storm had other plans.

"I would rather not be here when guests head downstairs." Her lips quivered, face still buried in Meera's shoulder.

"Okay, love. One, two, three..." Meera braced her arms under Sylvie's shoulders and pulled her up, steadying her on her feet. They walked together up the steps until they reached Sylvie's room. Meera let go of Sylvie as she opened the door for her. The room was messier than she would have liked it to be, and the lingering scent of a candle still clung to the edges of the room. She tried to ignore it all as she lumbered over to her bed and curled up under the soft, warm sheets. Meera shut the door behind them and curled up next to her on the other side of the bed. They were silent for a while, staring at the ceiling in a silence that only reminded her of Ronan. Their unspoken moments together were some of her favorites. It was how she knew she could be herself with him. To just be with someone in that way felt more vulnerable than any other form of connection.

Tears rolled down her cheeks, but she didn't shun them as they trailed past her ear and dampened her hair. It was okay to be in pain; she had learned that by now. That no amount of running was going to change it or take it away. This was her home, and she would make it work, even if Ronan and his scorned wife showed up to places together when she was around.

The thought instantly sickened her, and she shook her head to rid her mind of it as Meera turned on her side.

"Should I make that list now?" she asked gently.

"Yeah," Sylvie whispered back. "I can help."

"I think you've given great ideas already. Maybe just rest and—"

"No." Sylvie sniffed, wiping her tears away. "No, I should help. I need to help. It's my only purpose and joy right now."

Meera seemed to be considering just how much of a fight she was willing to put up, but decided against it.

"All right. Let's get to work then." She sat up and made her way around the bed. "Get dressed and meet me in the front room."

"Okay." Sylvie sat up just as Meera stepped into the hall. A new type of silence fell over the room, the kind that isn't as settled as in the company of someone familiar or comfortable. It made her head feel heavy with the painful memories she now held, and a part of her wanted to tuck in for the rest of the day, stare at the walls, and revel in her pain. But there was something inside her that was not there just a year ago. It wasn't the new breaks or the pain of loss in its most devastating forms, it was drive. Something she had long forgotten was inside her after letting life's waves crash into her and pull her away from a life lived to the fullest.

She would not sink back into despair. She owed herself more than that and had made it too far to let anything stop her when she was running full speed ahead. The rest of the week, the drive carried her, and though she cried at night, she was ready to start a new day every morning. Her family was by her side, cheering her on, giving her the hope she had once thought dead and gone.

Though she was broken, she was no longer incapacitated. If anything, she was even more motivated to love from a place of sincerity and understanding for people of all walks of life: their pains, their purposes, their highs and lows.

She was better for the pain and worked despite it because it had robbed her for too many years, and she had resolved that it wouldn't any longer.

After the previous round of guests left, weeks went by without anyone reserving a room. There was only a month left of the winter season and a bill was coming up. Once they had predicted, it would be no problem at all. And it wouldn't have been, had their trend of guests continued.

Meera called a meeting to discuss the situation.

"I don't understand. We had a great time with the last guests." Sylvie pinched her chin, shaking her head. June had joined the meeting, looking over Meera's other shoulder at the computer screen.

"Well, no one from the last round has left reviews for us." Meera pointed out, finger pressed, to the comment section of their page.

"But, how could that be? Everyone said they would when we were by the fire during that storm." June's brows tensed, her small nose lowering as she pressed her knuckles to her lips.

"They went into town after the storm on the last day of their stay. Maybe someone like Gertrude or something decided to badmouth what we're doing here?" Meera grimaced, uncertainty in her voice as much as there was spite.

Sylvie knew that feeling well, and it was silent for a second, as she chewed on her cheek.

"What are we gonna do?" June finally asked the question no one had wanted to think about because they had worked so hard to make it to here.

Sylvie swallowed the knot in her throat, unsure of the repercussions of the decision she knew was right. The one that meant they all are safe and secure. After one more beat of silence, she took a step back from the group and shakily declared, "We have to shut North Star Bed and Breakfast down."

CHAPTER 13
What Are You Doing Here?

"Sylvie, that can't be the answer." Meera shook her head, closing her laptop and turning to her.

"It's the only thing I can think of to ensure no one loses any money to keep this place afloat. Clearly, the townspeople still despise this place and don't want anything to do with it. Especially now that they clearly know about Ronan's and my affair."

"You don't know that for sure, Mom."

"Well, I'm not going to stay somewhere that I'm not wanted. I can't have a bed and breakfast that summons the gossipers to share the dirty details of my personal life to every guest that finds their way to Starwood. It's not fair to the guests, nor is it fair to me."

"I think you should sleep on it, Sylvie. I can find other options to promote the bed and breakfast. Our service and your love are really what give this place its draw. Not some nosey townspeople with nothing better to do with their lives than sit around gossiping about people they don't even really know."

"I don't know, Meera. Maybe we should just stop fighting fate for once."

"This isn't fate. You, owning this place, that's fate. We aren't giving up."

"Yeah, Mom. We won't let you."

Sylvie sat back against one of the long couches in the front room, thinking it over as she studied the patterns in the rug on the floor. After a moment, she looked up, searching both of their faces. There was only love in their eyes, only a drive to do what she had always wanted to do: to help her bring to life her passions and see their growth, too.

"All right. You have one month. But if business doesn't pick up, we're closing for the rest of the next few seasons until this thing blows over in the town."

The two of them looked between each other for a moment then back to Sylvie.

"I'm in." Meera stuck her hand out.

"Me, too." June laid her hand on top of Meera's, and they raised their brows at Sylvie's hesitation.

"Fine." Sylvie shook her grin. "I'm in, too."

She piled her hand on top of theirs.

Meera leaned in, eyes smiling. "Ladies, we're gonna save North Star."

She confidently beamed, and they broke away from the huddle, hands raising in agreement.

Over the next few weeks, Meera got to work on a new marketing strategy while June took baked goods to every business in the mainland, spreading the news of the bed and breakfast and its home away from home feel. Sylvie would make continual appearances in town to attempt to rebuild any broken relationships due to the scandal. Clearly she had been wronged, betrayed by Ronan, but the town was taking his side.

No one would so much as look her way when she greeted them, and it was the worst rejection to endure day in day out. But she did it, trying to bond with people by bringing fresh vegetables and fruits from their greenhouse that had grown through the winter because they had such a fantastic set-up. Still, most people wouldn't give her the time of day. Only some, the ones that liked what she brought them, would share some kindness, but they'd never go as far as to tell others to do the same.

She was basically shunned, and regardless of what she did, it seemed as though she only worsened it. The most frustrating part of it all was that Ronan's business seemed to be flourishing. His parking lot was always chocked full of people, and tours were constantly being given around town by men in suits and name tags. Clearly, their little drama had all but affected him. And he'd made no attempt to reach out to her about anything, either.

Not that really mattered. If anything, he was only listening to her orders. But still, it hurt to know that he didn't even try to apologize for being such a scumbag. She was only angry at him, never wanting to even see who was dropping River off every morning, though June had mentioned it was River's grandmother who brought her to work in the mornings.

Each day felt less hopeful than the one before, and in the final week of the winter season, Sylvie called every staff member into a meeting.

"Thank you all so much for being so incredible. Everything you've done for me and for this place has not gone unnoticed by any of our guests, and certainly not me. I'm forever grateful for your sacrifices and dedication." She forced herself to swallow, even though the dry patch in the back of her throat was growing.

All eyes were on her as she panned across the room, trying to find the words to thank and fire each person who had been so integral in making the place a success in the first place. "That being said, I also understand you all have lives. Things you want to get to, and possibly things you gave up to be here. Considering the way everything has been going for us, I think we should put a pause on the bed and breakfast, at least for the next few seasons."

The chatter began, confusion and sadness carried through the air like a devastating song. Sylvie fought back tears as she clapped once to regain their attention. "This is not a reflection of your work that has been more than satisfactory, but of external issues that I unknowingly created. I deeply apologize from the bottom of my heart, and I hope everyone can join us for the reopening at the end of the year."

She could tell this was a big ask and knew it was hard for anyone to just wait on a job. Even if they enjoyed the way her business was run, it didn't mean they had the ability to stay without pay. She looked to Meera, uncertain of how to continue. Her friend gently nodded, assuring her that everything would be okay. And even though she wasn't sure if it would be, she wanted to believe.

She inhaled through her nose, straightened her back as she looked deeply into the eyes of everyone she had grown to call family. "I understand if that's not possible and understand if you want to quit right now to find another option. Either choice is acceptable, and I will still be eternally grateful for the love and care you've sown into this place thus far. You all are my home, regardless of where you go."

The entire room was silent, the crackling fire in the dining room the only thing audible for the few seconds that followed. She felt as though they represented hours and days and months that every single person had given their all to. She would rather not be the bearer of bad news, but if this was what it had come to, they deserved to know the truth.

Meera stood up from her seat and took Sylvie's side, looking out at everyone, still clearly processing it all.

"We will give shining recommendation letters to anyone who needs them. Lunch is on us today, so please enjoy it." Meera pointed to June standing in the back with Lucy on her hip. June nodded before setting the needle down on the record player. Music filled the space, and chatter built like a crowded restaurant. Sylvie watched only for a moment longer before she couldn't take the sad sight before her.

She broke away from Meera and headed up the stairs to her room, but no one followed. They knew a broken heart couldn't always be cured with the comfort of friends.

And her heart was broken in more ways than one, for more reasons than she cared to think about.

Sylvie laid in bed for most of the day, wrapped up in the comfort of the warm sheets, listening to the hustle of everyone still hard at work downstairs. As far as she knew, no one had quit on the spot, but she wouldn't have been surprised if everyone had walked out. What she was expecting them to do was erroneous, and she knew it. It was her fault for not conducting her business better—personal and professional.

She watched the sunlight rotate through the sky most of the day, attempting not to fall into old habits of defeat and dismal thinking. Just as the moon shone brightly at the apex of the sky, and the North Star flickered for the first time, her eyes finally gave up fighting the tears inching their way to the surface.

They flowed down in hot streams, dampening her pillow and providing little solace for the aches throughout her body. The repercussions of everything truly hitting her all at once. She had nothing to fall back on if this failed, nothing to distract her sadness from sneaking up behind her. It loomed in the corner of her room just as Meera opened the door, shunning it away with her sunshine as she closed the door behind her and sat on the edge of the bed.

"I'd so hoped we could have stayed open this year." She softly spoke, as if speaking loudly might evoke something much sadder than the silence between them.

"Yes," Sylvie croaked, trying desperately not to sound

feeble. Yet, she felt all the more weak after hearing her shaking voice.

"We will open again." Meera turned her head to her, lowering her brows over her round eyes, filled with such sincerity she could convince just about anyone to believe anything. But Sylvie wasn't anyone, and she knew when hope was speaking rather than fact. "You don't believe me?"

"I hate it when you read my mind." Sylvie sniffed, a little scared that she might actually have some impossible powers. Though if she actually had powers, certainly she would have used them to save North Star.

"Well, I wouldn't have to if you actually said what was on it instead of keeping everything locked inside."

"I have my reasons..."

"We all do, but that doesn't make it okay."

"I don't think much would make this okay, Meera." Sylvie sat up, not wanting to take her frustrations out on Meera but unable to stop her tone from turning sour. "Saying what I'm thinking now will only make it hurt worse."

"Maybe so, but speaking your mind also means that people can get closer to you. You don't always have to be the strong one, Sylvie. You must be brave, of course. But always strong?" She shook her head. "An impossible feat."

Sylvie broke down at her friend's words, releasing her somehow from the years she'd spent bottling up pieces of her heart like they were inconveniences to be dealt with at a later time. Now, they were here, falling from her eyes and rattling her bones as she shook in Meera's arms. The world was a little upside down for Sylvie, but somehow from that angle, she could see everything right. She knew, maybe not that day or next, or even the one after it, but one day, she would be whole again. One brave step at a time.

Thankfully, for the rest of the week, she was able to get out of bed each morning and put on a brave face. Inside, she was repairing years worth of disregarded emotions, but on the outside, she was working to ensure that when and if North Star reopened, it would be ready for success.

Days went by and with each one, she felt a deeper sadness set in; the slowly declining staff, the sheets over furniture, and the last of the items in the kitchen being disposed of, all made her feel the weight of her loss that much greater.

Ronan would drift into her mind every so often and instead of pushing him away, she'd talk to Meera.

"He's an example of someone who can't own up to his emotions," she'd say, or they'd cry together about the loss of a potential love she thought she was growing or laugh about how silly their world really was at the moment.

But something was different, something refreshing and bright. She was able to laugh in the face of her pain and smile despite its aching presence. Throughout the final week of her dreams slowly dying, her heart was repairing at an unprecedented rate. With her family by her side, she knew she would be okay. No matter the outcome of North Star, her love life, or anything else that might seek to bring trials in her life.

Meera, June, and Lucy woke Sylvie up with breakfast in bed.

"Last day."

"Oh, you guys didn't have to do this."

"We did. You're our hero. You followed your heart, and no matter the outcome, you gave everything to see your dreams come to life." June beamed as she sat the tray on Sylvie's lap. Lucy crawled up into the bed next to her, mostly to beg for a chocolate chip off the top of her chocolate croissant.

"Here." Sylvie split the entire croissant in half and handed it to her. Her bright-green eyes lit up brightly, as if to ask her mother for permission.

"Let Nana eat her breakfast, Luce."

Lucy pouted, red lips stuck out as far as she could manage.

"It's fine, sweetie. I won't eat this all, anyhow." Sylvie assured her, and June shook her head with a soft smile.

"All right, you can eat, Lucy." She sat at the edge of the bed as Lucy squealed with such delight.

It made Sylvie wish she could be a child for a day. Only once, so she could experience that level of joy over the simplest things.

Meera sat on the other end of the bed, and they all enjoyed chatting about the memories they had made during their time in Starwood. The sun rose in the sky, shining beams through the room and splashing gold patterns on the Luis blue walls.

It was time to start the final day at North Star for a long time, perhaps forever.

With uncertainty on their heels, the girls headed downstairs, bracing themselves for the day ahead. Sylvie felt their strength combined with hers as they tended to the checklist Lyla had emailed to them to make sure everything was in order. When they reached the foyer, they were each assigned tasks, splitting up to accomplish them.

Sylvie was tasked with weeding the gardens and covering them with warming sheets to keep everything secure from any future storms. There was still a bit of time left in the winter season, and it was still possible that in this climate, weather could destroy crops in the greenhouse.

Better to be safe than sorry, Lyla noted in brackets on the printed out copies of her email.

Sylvie crossed through the ground level and into one of the closets with the gloves, straw hats, and gardening aprons. She wasn't sure what all she would need, but she knew the gardeners kept everything in one place, just by the door that led to the greenhouse.

After fastening the apron around her waist, sliding on the gloves, and sticking the hat under her arm, she examined the garden section of the list in hand. Gardening was not something that she was unfamiliar with, she did it as often as she could on her terrace in New York. But the scale, at which the garden she would be tending to, frightened her a little.

Although it scared her, she was not hesitant, not like she used to be when things felt too big to handle. She was prepared for anything.

As she headed out the door, eyes locked to the list, she stepped across the stone pathway in the direction of the greenhouse. But before she could reach it, she ran full speed ahead into something that shifted upon her colliding with it. Shock and embarrassment sent her backward, and she searched over what had been stuck in her path. Though as she registered it, she realized that it was not something at all, but rather, someone. More specifically, someone she had hoped she'd never see again.

With as much bravery as her waning frame could muster, she tensed, creases forming between her brows, frown turning down the edges of her displeased mouth. "What are you doing here?"

CHAPTER 14
The Truth Hurts

"I actually came to speak to you." Gertrude Price spoke faintly, something Sylvie hadn't known her capable of. She crossed her arms over her chest, wondering what intentions hid behind her seemingly harmless words. There was something different about her, though, something Sylvie couldn't deny. It was a certain meekness, a willowy version of her once persnickety obstinance.

"Well, I don't have much time. I'm sure you've heard by now. It's the last day for North Star, so you'll have to excuse me." She intended to brush past her, but Gertrude stepped in front of her again, toiling with her fingers nervously. Sylvie had half the brain to ask her to move. Anger quaked within her, but Gertrude looked down, readily about to accept the unkind words Sylvie had been dying to deliver to her since her stint at the grand opening.

She lowered her shoulders, studying the lines of Gertrude's weathered face, unable to determine her real purpose for showing up on that day of all days. Her overdramatic shiver and pleading gray eyes locked onto Sylvie's, and she sighed with annoyance.

She was a pain to deal with, but ultimately, Sylvie had wronged her unintentionally, and she was determined to make it right.

"Come inside." She turned back toward the side door. "You have five minutes, but only because I owe you that much."

She thought she saw her cock her head upon agreeing but ignored it, heading to the bed and breakfast. As she reached the side door, she looked over her shoulder. Gertrude stood immovable still, shock written across her face.

"Are you coming?" Sylvie called, and it was as if her words snapped Gertrude out of her trance. She practically hopped forward, clicking her heels across the stone until she was by Sylvie's side.

Sylvie turned the gold knob, cool beneath her fingers as she pulled it open with hesitancy. What more could Gertrude Price want? She got all she desired with North Star closing indefinitely. And surely, she wasn't here to rub in the fact that her son-in-law used her for some strange emotional affair.

They crossed through to the front room, but Sylvie left both doors open, ushering her to the couch beside the fireplace. She sat opposite of her before texting Meera to bring her some tea and two mugs.

They were silent for a moment as Gertrude looked around the room, observing it with a blank face. Not but a minute more, Meera came barreling into the room, tea, and mugs on a tray. Both Sylvie and Gertrude looked at her sudden appearance.

"Thank you." Sylvie nodded implicitly at Meera's vacant blinking.

"My pleasure," Meera finally said, placing the tray on the coffee table and exiting the room much quieter than she came.

"Tea?" Sylvie held a mug under the hot porcelain kettle.

"Yes, please." Gertrude composed herself, straightening her back as she watched Sylvie pour and eventually hand her the cup. It was silent for a moment more as they sipped, then Sylvie couldn't take it any longer, so she took a breath to speak.

"So—" As she spoke, Gertrude did as well, but she shook her head, waving her hand for Sylvie to continue.

"So, what brings you to North Star today? Ms. Price?"

"We'll, like I said, I'm here to speak to you."

"You did say that, didn't you." Sylvie intentionally checked her watch before Gertrude continued.

Gertrude clicked her tongue, setting her tea down on the table before looking into the fire like it was displaying a memory. "It was all a misunderstanding."

"What?" Sylvie confusion had her heart skipping like it knew before she did what Gertrude meant.

"Ronan is not married." She pursed her lips like she had little time for incompetence.

"He—"

"My daughter, Lily…" A tear glistened in the corner of

her eye as she looked away. "She was killed in a car crash not long after River was born."

The weight of this story, alone, turned Sylvie's blood cold. She exhaled a shaky breath through slightly parted lips, setting her mug down on the coffee table across from Gertrude's.

"She was driving with Ronan's father. They were going out to get him a gift for Father's Day. There was a tropical storm. The roads were flooded." She sighed so fervently it turned Sylvie's stomach.

"A perfect recipe for the type of tragedy that befell us that evening. Of course, I welcomed Ronan and my granddaughter into our home, and they've stayed with us ever since. He could live anywhere, but he knows how special River is to me. She reminds me so much of Lily. So determined and bright. And that hair." She smiled deeply, making her seem more human. "We'll, that wild red hair is all Lily."

"I'm so sorry." Sylvie mustered, latched on to every word.

"I'm not here for your sympathy, Ms. Blythe." She regained her cold exterior once more, but something about it wasn't so menacing anymore. It was like the coverings over plants in the winter. She knew something much more was hidden beneath its surface. "I'm here because I want to ask you, implore you, to speak with Ronan."

"I don't understand..."

"I have never, in the entire time since the accident, seen my son-in-law as happy as he was the moment you got into town. I noticed the change immediately, which made me realize what I had done, the part I had played in breaking the two of you up. I thought I was losing him, and in turn, my granddaughter. But I see now how much he cares for you."

"*Cares*?"

She nodded once.

"Then, why are you the one here and not him?"

"Ms Blythe, Ronan is a gentleman. He figured he should respect your wishes to disassociate from him."

"Look..." Sylvie sat forward. "I apologize for everything your family has been through, but his lack of communication when it counted is what got us here. You just helped our relationship reach its endpoint much sooner than I was willing to push it."

"He's leaving."

"He's what?"

"He's going to leave tonight with River. They're moving someone further inland."

A pang of something horrible, hit Sylvie like a tidal wave. "W-what? Why? His father's business is here."

"I told him that already, believe me. I've tried just about everything except—"

"Except begging me to make him stay."

"Yes, but it's more than that. He's doing this for you."

"How could you be so certain?" Sylvie really wanted the answer to make sense, but deep down, she knew she couldn't get her hopes up.

"He said he was leaving to give your business a chance. He's dominating the market. With him gone, the only way for visitors to stay in Starwood would be through your bed and breakfast."

Sylvie sat with the truth in her lap, looking down at it with not a clue how to deal with this new information. How could he be so frustratingly selfless? It wouldn't make sense unless he too had an ache in his heart every time he thought about her and pain running through the happiest memories they shared.

"He can't leave," she barely said before looking up at Gertrude. Guilt shivered through her as she recounted yelling at him about his wife, who had died years ago.

It all made sense. The town shunning her for being so classless and rash, without knowing that she was completely in the dark about everything.

Still, it hurt her to know how much she had hurt him, how much she had hurt the town.

Even so, was it worth begging him to stay? Wouldn't it only hurt him worse? And if she did convince him to remain in Starwood, what would their relationship look like?

Her heart skipped at the thought. Another preemptive leap that she had little time to address as she stood. Gertrude observed her, seemingly unsure of what she might do. Sylvie was just as uncertain. How could she decide whether to let the man of her dreams go, or beg him to stay and let everything she's wanted since her youth crumble to ruin around her?

After everything, he hadn't even attempted to reach out to her. What if he didn't feel the same for her, and every time he looked at her, he would only be reminded of his losses? She couldn't do that to him.

But what if the connection between them was beckoning their hearts, pointing them toward a life better than they'd ever dreamed? Was it brave of her to try, or was she trying to be strong for all the wrong reasons?

"I'll see you out," Sylvie said, but she felt distant from her words, and Gertrude walked with her to the front door wordlessly.

"So, you'll speak to him?" she weakly asked as Sylvie opened the door, eyes fixed nowhere in particular.

"Goodbye, Gertrude." She pressed her lips together as she closed the door in her face. It wasn't on purpose, her curt dismissal or the way she couldn't focus on anything.

She wasn't sure what to make of her emotions and didn't know when they would reach equilibrium. So, she leaned against the front doors, biting her lip as her mind swirled into a jumbled, disoriented mess.

"Mom." June was in front of her before she realized it, forest green eyes concerned and searching.

"Yes, honey?" Sylvie finally focused on something just as the words spilled from her lips. An envelope, the size of a small dish, rested between June's hesitant fingers. "What's this?"

"It's something I shouldn't have kept from you." Her usually chirpy tone was shaky and remorseful.

Sylvie's head shifted into a new gear. Someone she loved needed her help. That was most important. That took precedence above all confusing drama.

"What is it?" Her brows tensed and lowered, studying

June's dark lashes that hit her cheeks as her eyes looked down at their feet.

"A letter."

"I can see that. What's in it?" June shook her head, handing it over as Sylvie's heart began to ache from pumping overtime. She took it in her hands, and her fingers danced over the ridges of the envelope as she slipped her finger underneath its opening. Slowly, the peeled back the triangular piece and shimmied out a lined notebook page, folded neatly.

Her stomach tightened with each undoing, as she floated the paper with her shaking hands. What could possibly garner this much mystery and tangible tension in the air?

Before she could get too far skimming what looked to be a handwritten note, she saw the greeting.

"Dear Sylvia May," and she knew exactly why June had kept it from her. She glanced up at June's dismay, so saddened and disappointed in herself.

"Why did you keep this from me?" Sylvie asked, taking her daughter's chin softly between her thumb and index.

June shook her head out of Sylvie's grasp, eyes beginning to shimmer with tears.

"I thought I was helping you. I didn't know he would leave. I—"

"It's okay, don't worry. Okay?"

She blinked wet lashes at her as her brows tightly pulled together. "You're not upset?"

"Of course not. How could I be? You were only doing

what you thought was right. And honestly, Junie, I would have done the same thing."

She pulled June into a hug, hoping it soothed her guilty conscience. They stood there for a moment until Lucy called from the top of the stairs.

"Mommy!" She drew out the word like a song, and June pulled away, wiping her tears with a half-grin.

"Yes?" June mimicked back.

"Peter Pan just fell from the roof of Barbie manor."

June breathed a laugh through her nose, exchanging a look with Sylvie, who was instantly taken back to June's childhood. She'd always find ways to get her mother to play dolls just a little longer with her, a lot like little Lucy who waited patiently for her mother to respond.

"Okay, baby. I'll be up in a second."

"Okay..." Lucy trailed for a second, her tiny feet patting up a few stairs before stopping. "But hurry because I think he forgot how to fly!"

"Okay, Lucy." June chuckled before grabbing Sylvie's arm. "Do you need me to stay with you while you read the letter?"

"No, no. I think Peter Pan forgetting to fly is definitely a bigger crisis than this silly letter." She laughed, pulling June into one last hug.

"Mommy!" Lucy called, and June pulled away from Sylvie, rolling her eyes in amusement as she headed for the stairs.

"Coming!" she called.

Sylvie watched her until she turned up the next flight of stairs, then her eyes trailed back to the paper still in her hand. Her chest rose and fell with a deep sigh that did nothing for her frayed nerves.

"All right," she whispered to herself, forcing her eyes to the words on the page.

"Dear Sylvia May,

There are no words to describe the level of remorse I feel for not telling you my entire story. You are kind and patient for never digging into it, even when I know I shut you out. For that, I am sorry. And I apologize for a million other things that I got wrong with us, but I won't apologize for pursuing you.

You were and are the best thing that's happened to me in a very, very long time. I don't pretend to assume you'd ever wish to speak to me again, but I implore you to at least hear me out. I owe you an explanation, one that will not suffice in a letter.

Meet me at the lighthouse on Saturday at sunset. If you don't come, I'll leave you alone for good. I only want you to be happy and get everything you deserve.

All the best,

Ronan Ashton"

Sylvie blinked away the blurry vision that had set in when her tears began to flow at a steady pace. They rolled down her cheeks and dropped onto the page as she rested against the wall, sinking to the floor in a slow defeat. She had missed the mark weeks ago. He thought she wanted nothing to do with him.

At the time, that was mostly true. This letter would have confused her, and if she had gone, she might have found out sooner that there was more to his life she didn't yet understand.

Now, it was too late.

She listened to the click of the grandfather clock's chains reaching the late afternoon chime. The bells rang through the empty bed and breakfast as she looked through the window at the top of the grand staircase. Thick, fluffy clouds slowly passed by as her thoughts slowed down to a more manageable rate. Just weeks ago, Ronan had meant the world to her, but he had also been withholding vital details of himself. It was a risk even reaching out to him. But she owed him at least the permission to stay. Regardless of how his business had affected hers, she didn't want him to give up his father's business just because he felt guilty. He didn't deserve that.

She pulled out her phone before she could stop herself, fingers frantically scrolling through her contacts until she stopped on his name. What was she doing? She should let him live in peace, but apparently, that's not what she really felt because she was pressing his name and hitting the call option like her hands had a mind of their own.

It rang many times before going to voicemail, but just as the chime beeped for her to record her message, she got too nervous and hung up. What would she even say to him? She grabbed the letter off the floor, skimming back over the page until her eyes stuck on one thing. Hastily, she pulled her phone back into her line of sight and typed out a message to him.

"Meet me at the lighthouse in an hour.
— Sylvie"

CHAPTER 15

Wish Me Luck

It was early evening by the time Sylvie was ready. With only ten minutes to spare, she would need to sprint across her land and up the hill to the lighthouse overlooking the ocean. Her mind felt as endless as that view, thoughts rising and falling like the wild tide and whipping waves. She clipped in her last earring, gold with a single dangling pearl.

The first instinct she had after messaging Ronan was to get changed. Perhaps, it was because she didn't know what to do with her shaking hands, or there could have been something much deeper. Feelings she'd thought needed to be laid to rest swelled in her chest as she adjusted her waves in the mirror, clipping strands of hair back on either side of her face.

The winter sun waned in the sky and set her room to a hue of gold as she finished slipping on her pale teal dress. It was embroidered with pastel purple flowers at the top, collecting at the waist with goofy quarter sleeves that cinched at her elbow then billowed out again. It was a soft flowing dress with a thick underskirt to protect her from the cold winter air, no doubt still fluttering through the trees as the sun set.

She checked the time right as she slipped on a pair of rubber boots, preparing to trudge through the thick grass. It was nearly an hour since her message to Ronan, and she wanted to avoid being late to meet him.

Even if he never showed, the risk of asking him was worth it, though she desperately hoped he would.

As she stepped out of her bedroom, a floorboard creaked on her right. Lyla hovered in the hallway with a toothy grin.

"This place is impressive." She cheekily raised her brows as Sylvie ran to her, enveloping her in a tight hug.

"Why are you here?"

"Well, I heard the business was struggling, and I just wanted to see how you were doing," she said into her shoulder before Syvlie pulled away to look into her eyes.

"I'm okay," she whispered sincerely as Meera and June stepped out of one of the rooms further down the hall.

"You're going to meet him?" June called, bright eyes glowing gleefully when she saw how dressed up her mother had gotten.

"Meeting who?" Lyla's eyes softened as she looked between them.

"You're meeting Ronan?" Meera asked and Lyla blinked in an exaggerated manner.

"Ronan? I thought you guys were done?"

"It's a long story." Sylvie bit the corner of her lip as Meera and June reached them.

"She has a really good reason to meet with him." June told both Meera and Lyla, who seemed utterly unconvinced of that fact.

"I'm kind of running on a bit of a time crunch, though." Sylvie grimaced, baring her teeth as she took a step back.

"Wait!" June reached between the group, grabbing her mother and pulling her into another hug. "You got this."

Two more sets of arms wrapped around them.

"You're brave," Meera whispered.

"And you make dreams come true," Lyla added as the warmth of their bodies enveloped Sylvie so deeply that she felt their support at the very center of her being. Perhaps, she had everything she needed all along to make her life the way she wanted. All it took was the love of her family to cheer her on.

As they all pulled away, Sylvie took one last look at their faces, admiring how much she had grown to be comforted by the simplicity of their mere presence.

"Wish me luck." She shrugged, stepping away from them as they chirped their well-wishes.

Her feet were light but urgent, heading down the stairs and padding across the foyer. With as much purpose as she could muster, she slipped out the front door, closing it behind her as a sharp draft whistled through the air.

Despite its persistence to make her turn around, she stomped down the snow-covered steps and crossed to the open field next to the bed and breakfast. Up the hill she went, slogging through slippery tall grass that brushed past her on every side. It was freezing, but she barely noticed as she made her way through the golden light, up to the towering white lighthouse before her. She caught her breath just as she broke through into the clearing where it resided, her heart pounding in every limb as she clutched her chest.

"Calm down, Sylvie," she whispered to herself, trying not to focus on what if's and instead, forced her feet to take her to the front of the lighthouse. Somehow, the walk around it felt longer than usual. It was as if each step she took made the distance grow even more.

Still, she pushed forward, ignoring everything inside her begging her not to go. That it would only hurt worse to see his perfect face again and hear his soft words explaining things she already knew. It was too much for her to bear, but she would do it if it meant that the even smaller voice inside her, pushing her on, would soon shut up.

One way or another, she was going to put an end to the questions, doubting, confusion, and longing. All equally wrapped up into a package she had hoped she wouldn't need to open for much later in her life when little regrets would start to creep in.

Too much had been left like this in her life. She was determined not to continue doing the same thing, over and over. She had made so much progress with her healing, and now was not the time to retreat.

As she rounded the lighthouse, her stomach clenched, grew tight, and the eyes rounded. The golden light framed

Ronan's silhouette that faced the ocean as the wind rustled his perfect hair. He turned toward her the moment her foot took another step closer in the cold, crunchy grass just beginning to freeze from the dropping temperature.

"Good evening." He had a soft grin that made her feel warmer than the sun could in the winter air.

"You came." She swallowed, wishing she had said something else. Something smoother or more direct.

His grin widened, eyes twinkling like the stars beginning to make their way into the sky.

"Of course, I came." He took a step toward her.

"You're leaving?" She hated the sad tone her voice curled into as his face dropped, lips turning down, bright eyes glowing past her for a moment.

"I thought it was what you wanted."

"I never wanted you to leave." She looked down at her muddied boots before forcing herself to be brave. "The second I knew what you had been hiding from me, all I wanted you to do was go after me."

"Gertrude told me what she had done, coming to visit you like that." He shook his head, grimacing a little. "She should have talked to me first... I don't want you to worry about me."

Sylvie cocked her head. "I don't want you to worry about me."

"What?"

"You're leaving town to give North Star a chance?"

He sighed despondently. "Yes, but—"

"No buts. It's not fair for either of us to give up our

careers for the other." She clenched her jaw, angry at his defiance. "You don't owe me anything."

The hurt in his eyes showed through like lightning in the night sky. "How could you say that?"

"Because you don't."

"But I do."

"No, you don't."

"Yes, I do."

Sylvie grimaced, tightening her fists into balls. "Why? Why can't you just let me go, Ronan?"

He tensed his brows, eyes searching hers. He gave no answer, no response as his lips pressed together.

"I've tried so hard to let you go, why can't you do the same?"

"Because, Sylvia May—"

"I told you not to call me that ever again—"

"I love you." His words rang through the air, making everything freeze. Even the ocean behind him seemed to quiet at his proclamation. This was the first time he had properly said it. Sure, there were near-misses here and there. And perhaps, she knew his feelings all along, but to hear them come from his mouth, soaked in such sincerity, made her eyes water with realization.

In her pause, he seemed to worry, his eyes lowered as his pink lips parted. "I won't apologize for—"

"What took you so long?" She cut him off, smiled a mile wide, practically shaking from the rush of his words. He tensed his brows, cocking his head with an amusement that made him even more irresistible than he already was.

"I didn't want to rush anything...but..."

"But?"

"But I think I've loved you from the moment I met you. The moment you clumsily ran into me with that bike of yours and complained about the flaws of my business to me." He laughed, rubbing a hand over his stubbly chin. "You're the best person I know." "

His words weren't making sense, yet at the same time, they were far too clear. He had loved her since before they had even truly known each other. Questions pricked her mind as words fell from her mouth that felt far from her.

"Why didn't you tell me?" She barely spoke above a whisper.

"I should have told you. I should have gone after you, the second you left my office, and shouted it through the town until you believed how desperately I did...and do *love you*."

There those words were again, hanging in the air like a question she'd been ignoring.

"Ronan," Sylvie breathed, uncertain of how to answer something so deeply connected to the core of her. There was one problem, a flaw with the way her words were forming, and it was not that she didn't feel the same; it was that she *did*.

After everything and maybe despite it, she was not confused anymore.

"I love you," she whimpered back, and he took a step closer. Somehow, those confessions were still not enough to end the dread still troubling her with its worst scenarios. Before he could get too close, she reached up, pressing her hand to his firm chest. "But..."

"But?" He was hanging onto her words, eyes shifting between hers, begging for her to continue.

She took another step closer to him this time, heart drumming like the beginning of a song. Her right hand was still holding him back, but it didn't seem to deter his longing for her.

That draw between them, the gravitational pull of something beyond words, held them steadily as her hand remained the barrier between them. He held her arm in place as if her pulling away would ruin him, and she thought it might ruin her, too.

As much as she wanted everything with him, their two worlds to collide and never stop, she couldn't brush her deepest worries to the side. Not if she hoped to make their love last.

"Communication was a thorn in my marriage's side. I believe it caused the end. We lacked it, we had it in all the wrong ways, and eventually, we had nothing at all. I don't want that. Don't want to go through that all over again. It would be a waste for me to have come here, to have started this new life, and just slip right back into my old one. I want this to work because I really like you." She pursed her upturned lips. "I really love you, and I want you—"

Before she could utter another word, Ronan cupped her face with his warm, strong hands and pulled her mouth to his. His soft sweet lips were fervent, shooting fireworks off at the spark of their collision with hers. That fire spread through her, lighting up every nerve in her body as she clung tightly to him, never wanting him to let go or pull away.

He was more than she had ever known—more loving, more steady, more intentional. If a kiss could break curses in fairy tales, she thought, certainly this kiss would end every one of them. Her heart grew, as if his had always been what was missing in hers. Somehow, their love had made them both whole. They held each other for a moment as their lips pulled apart gently.

"You deserve the world, Sylvia May, and I intend to give that to you." His breath called the chill against her skin before he stepped back from her. At first, she was confused, unsure of what he was doing until he reached in his pocket, bending down until one of his knees rested on the short wheat-colored grass.

A small high-pitched gasp escaped her as she looked at the bolt in his hand. He held it up like a ring, presenting it earnestly, his cheeks a shade of pink that she'd never seen them grow.

"This is a bolt that I've had in my pocket since the day we broke ground on North Star Bed and Breakfast. You used to tell me how much you believed in fate. That the North Star was guiding you, like it did the sailors. North was where your dreams were, where your love could be expressed. I've thought about it for as long as I've known this fact about you. And I wondered, what was my North Star, my dream, my ambition? I can honestly say that it took me until just now to realize it."

He looked up at the sky, a blanket of deep blue, covered in bright twinkling stars. She looked at it with him for a moment, resting her eyes on the brightest one. The one she could point out even with her eyes closed. Then, his glowing blues were back on her, and she felt the warmth of his smile as he shook his head.

"Sylvia May, you are my North Star. Wherever you go, I want to follow you. For the rest of my life, I wish to be with you. I intend to spend every moment of time I have left on this earth, trying to make you as happy as you make me."

Her eyes welled up with fresh tears as she let out a laugh of disbelief. She knew what he was asking, but just wanted to hear the sweet words fall from his perfect lips. "What are you saying?"

"Sylvia May Blythe, will you marry me?"

She searched his face for a moment, knowing the answer was deeply rooted inside of her. Somehow, it had been there all along, and it was as if she had discovered the truth of just how intently her affections ran. Ronan Ashton was certainly a surprise, but love is rarely predictable. And she did love him. Truly, with all of her being, with every star in the sky, with every breath in her lungs.

"Yes." She nodded vehemently as he rose to embrace her. She buried her face in his flannel shoulder. "I will."

Undoubtedly, she knew, he was the one for her. Perhaps, their stars had aligned at the right time, at the time they needed each other the most. She would always need him the most, from then on, they were each other's North Star.

Epilogue

A Few Months Later

" I thought you wanted the flower arrangements out the back, Eleanor!" June called from down the hall, footsteps loud and frustrated as Sylvie's youngest daughter, Eleanor, directed foot traffic.

"This way, June. *This* way." She clapped, annoyance drenching her tone.

Meera was twisting beautiful braids around Sylvie's head as she sat in front of her vanity, pins in her mouth and flowers scattered atop the dresser in front of them.

"It really takes an army to put together a wedding in three months." Meera chuckled, and Sylvie relaxed her shoulders, which had been tense from all the shouting between her children downstairs.

"I think this is the loudest this bed and breakfast has been, and just last week, we had forty people staying here."

Sylvie bit her lower lip, placing a flower in Meera's open palm.

"Thank you," Meera wrapped the step of it around a bobby pin and placed it gently in another spot on Sylvie's head. "I think you just need to breathe, sweetie. Everything will be fine."

"The wedding is in an hour, and I don't even think any of our bridesmaids are ready."

"Let the maid of honor worry about that, Sylvie."

Sylvie blew out a heavy breath. "You're already doing so much, though."

Meera fasted one last flower, waving her hand dismissively before handing Sylvie a mirror to see the back. She spun her around in the chair, pointing out the braids wrapped round and round in an intricate pattern that looked like a fairy godmother had zapped into place. She loved it, loved the way the hairstyle made her hazel eyes pop.

Even the little white and blue flowers laid perfectly in the right areas.

"Do you like it?" Meera nervously fiddled with her fingers.

"I love it, Meera." Sylvie wanted to trace every pathway that the braids created around her freshly-curled hair. She settled on messing with the curled pieces that framed her face, wrapping one around her finger as she looked at herself in the mirror.

"I'm so glad!" Meera crouched down, hands on Sylvie's shoulders as she looked at her through the mirror. "You look absolutely stunning, Sylvie."

"All thanks to you." She placed a hand over top of one of Meera's.

"Could somebody, please, grab these instruments out of the walkway?! I *literally* almost broke an ankle!" Eleanor shouted to no one in particular, and Sylvie winced.

"That's my cue." Meera buzzed out of the room before she could offer to help. There was some commotion that followed, some indiscernible talking, clanking of instruments, and doors shutting. But within moments, Meera had somehow gotten everyone outside where they needed to be.

Everyone except for the boys, who Ronan had taken on a little fishing trip just a night before their wedding. He had said how much he wanted to get to know her boys better, so that was a big reason why he had to do it so late. Both of them had gotten in only two nights before the wedding, and they were groomsmen. Ronan insisted on it, even though he hadn't met them in person yet.

"You look..." The sound of a hand clapping to a muscular chest caused her to spin around.

"Ronan, you're not supposed to see me before the wedding. It's bad luck." Sylvie stood up, prepared to close the door on him, but he stopped it with his foot. His blue eyes cheekily grinning with a sparkle that never seemed to fade.

"You're all the luck I need." He stooped, his soft lips brushing against hers, freezing her in place and causing her to lean into him. It was instinctual at this point, the way they never could stay away from one another for too long. Even when they were in the same room, they seemed to gravitate toward one another like magnets.

He pulled away, inhaling deeply through his nose before he pressed the tip of it to hers.

"You really should go," she whispered as he pulled her closer to him.

He nodded, eyes dancing with hers, and her head began to spin.

"I'll see you out there," he finally said, softly tracing her cheek with his knuckle. Chills rose in the musky trail he left on her skin as he stepped back, still holding on to her hand.

Meera must have spotted him slowly backing away from the bottom of the steps because she began speaking in Telugu angrily.

"Ronan Ashton!" It was all either of them could make out.

His eyes went wide as he let go.

"I love you," he mouthed before sprinting back down the hallway.

Sylvie chuckled.

"At least you're still in your robe and not your dress." Meera huffed as she climbed the steps, scowling in the direction Ronan had run, probably considering whether to chase after him.

"At least." Sylvie sarcastically agreed, raising her brows as she turned on her heels.

"The girls are officially getting ready downstairs, and

the boys are now all in the green suite on level three."
Meera flurried around the room, gathering things together
and pulling Sylvie's wedding dress out of the closet.

"Thank you, Meera. You're a lifesaver."

"Not yet, I'm not, because we have forty minutes until
the wedding, and you still don't have your dress on."

Sylvie smirked, watching her unzip the dress bag.
Meera glanced over her shoulder, eyes narrowing.

"What's so funny?"

"Oh, it's nothing." She shook her head and grinned.
"You're sounding a lot like Lyla."

"You take that back, Sylvie. I'm nothing like her,"
Meera scoffed.

"Just keep telling yourself that, but I think you've
grown to be a little more organized at the very least..."

"Let's hope so, for your sake. You wouldn't want your
marketing lead slacking in that department." Meera pulled
Sylvie's dress from the dress bag, and Sylvie lost her train
of thought as she stared at it in awe.

She'd only tried it on once in the Nantucket boutique
just a month ago. It had been a long day, and everyone was
a bit fed up with shopping. She was walking past the
window and saw a dress on one of the mannequins toward
the back of the store. Turned out that it was just a size
larger than she needed.

One try on with the tailor present, and the rest was
history. Now floating toward her was the dress of her
dreams. Layers of sheer so dense it flowed like a Louis blue
waterfall. The sleeves were purely flouncy fabric, made to

scoop around the shoulders and highlighted her collar bones.

Meera guided it over to her, taking off the sheer corset piece with blue embroidered flowers that highlighted her waist. She unlaced the back of the dress, opening it up for Sylvie to step through. Fireworks were bursting within her chest and swirling around her stomach, making her hold her breath as she moved closer.

Just as she slipped off her robe and both her feet were securely in the opening of the dress, there was a knock at the door.

"One second!" Sylvie and Meera called in unison as they raised the dress to her hips.

Another knock resounded, Meera helped guide her arms through the armholes.

"Wait!" Meera called just as Lyla slipped through the doorway.

"Does *wait* mean nothing to you?" Meera grumbled, lacing up the back of the dress as Lyla beamed over at Sylvie.

"Oh, Sylvie, you're a vision!" Her lips quivered as she blotted away a tear in her typical dramatic fashion.

Sylvie pouted her smile to the side, trying to accept the compliment without teasing her.

"Would you help me with this, Lala?" Meera grunted.

Lyla put up a finger in front of her scowling face. "Stop calling me that, first of all..."

"And *second*?" Meera flatly prodded, causing Lyla to loudly sigh.

"Yes." She dropped her shoulders. "I can help you."

She scurried around Sylvie's billowing dress. Together, Meera and Lyla fastened the flowery corset layer of the dress before both crossing to the front of her to get a better look.

Their silent admiration was slightly embarrassing. Sylvie hadn't had a group admiring her this way since her first wedding. And she was four months pregnant, so it wasn't anything spectacular to shower praise on, not like this dress. She felt as beautiful as the girls made it seem she was. Everything really turned out so dreamy; the dress, the wedding, and the deep love between Ronan and her.

She tucked a curled strand of hair behind her ear, knowing her cheeks were reddening and trying to look down to hide it.

"Truly, this is the most gorgeous dress. But *you*, Sylvie, are absolutely transcendent."

Lyla leaned toward Meera. "She looks like she's glowing."

"Wow." Meera's round caramel eyes softened, and she nodded. "She does."

They continued to look her up and down for another minute.

When the pressure of being observed so intently had become overbearing, Sylvie clapped her hands together. "All right, that's enough."

She chuckled nervously as the girls rolled their affectionate eyes.

"Ronan won't be able to keep his eyes off you. That's

all I'll say." Lyla turned around, chin cocked toward her neck implicitly as she reached for the door handle. Before slipping out into the hall, she took one last look at Sylvie over her shoulder, making Sylvie take a shaky breath.

"Everyone is in position, is what I came to call you both. We're ready when the bride is." Her red lips softly turned up at the edges before she snuck back into the hall, shutting the door quietly behind her.

"Are you ready?" Meera whispered for no reason in particular. All Sylvie could think was she was trying not to make her any more nervous. But she wasn't really nervous, not like she was the first time she got married. She felt so sick that time that she couldn't even walk down the aisle without her head spinning.

Not this day, though. This day, she felt absolutely so sure about Ronan that it steadied any nerves that passed by about the many gazes focused on her. With a gentle breath, she blew out any lingering worries that she'd trip, or something embarrassing, in front of everyone. When she inhaled, she only let in the excitement, the sheer joy rooted in her harmonious love with Ronan.

She leaned in to Meera, taking her hand and squeezing it gently. "I'm more ready than I've ever been for anything."

Meera's eyes lit from within. "Then, let's get you out there."

She walked toward the door, and Sylvie followed behind, holding up the front of her dress with both hands, so she didn't trip on her way down the stairs. She could see through the front windows of the foyer, the rows of different chairs with colorful streams of ribbon on the corners and flowers down the aisle. As she neared the bottom of the steps, her bridesmaids lined up in order at the door.

Meera found her way to the back of the line as Sylvie brushed past the girls.

"Mom, you look stunning," June whispered, and Eleanor nodded in agreement.

"So pretty." River gleamed.

Lyla touched her arm affectionately as she passed by, and finally, she met Gertrude's silver eyes.

"Sylvie, you are the most beautiful bride I've seen in a very long time." The creases in her face deepened kindly as she reached for her hand. Sylvie took it, so thankful that Gertrude had agreed to be a part of the wedding. It felt like an olive branch, having her join them, knowing her presence would honor Ronan and River.

"Thank you." Sylvie lowered her brows sincerely before heading to the very back of the group.

It was then that she realized it—she hadn't chosen someone to walk her down the aisle. They didn't get time to do a rehearsal with the chaos of shutting the bed and breakfast down for a few days. She couldn't imagine what shutting it down for a whole year, like they had planned, would have been like.

Just as the doors opened for June to walk through, Sylvie grabbed Meera's arm and called Lyla to her. Lyla hurried to her side, and the three stood close together as the doors opened again for Eleanor to walk through.

"What's going on?" Lyla was the first to ask, but Meera waited just as intently as her.

"Will you guys walk me down the aisle?"

"I would be honored." Meera's eyes glistened as she linked her arm with Sylvie's.

"Me, too." Lyla sniffed, wrapping her arm around Sylvie's.

Having the two of them by her side was everything she had needed for a very long season of her life. She'd always need them in many ways, but this was the last time she'd need them in the way she had for so many years.

Her life was moving forward, and they would always be a part of it, but they had their own stories to make and adventures to take. So as they stepped up to those double doors, her heart beating like the wings she was about to spread, she looked on either side of her.

"I love you both."

"We love you," they echoed back just as the doors opened, and the salty breeze, carrying a beautiful instrumental, twirled around them.

Her feet were sure, softly treading across the porch. With each step, Sylvie's anticipation built. Knots tied themselves in the pit of her stomach as she braced herself for the grass. Sweat accumulated in the creases of her nervous palms, and her legs wobbled slightly as she stopped in front of the aisle.

The trees were strung with lanterns, and the sun was just beginning to set behind their glow. Wild flowers covered everywhere they could, causing the entire aisle to smell sweet and delicate.

Her nerves were at their peak until she looked up and met Ronan's pine blues, like beacons, and everything fell away.

The knots in her stomach untied, and feet found security in the lush grass, but heart thumped with the giddy certainty that she'd finally gotten it right.

With each step over the lush grass scattered with colorful flower petals, her eyes stayed glued to Ronan's. The closer she got to him, the better she could see his cheeks glistening with fresh tears. She wouldn't dare look away from him, though it caused her to tear up as well.

Everything within her swelled, tilting toward him like a tree in the wind. Nothing else mattered. Not the eyes of their guests of the midsummers night dream decor, cascading around them like a waterfall of flowers, not even the placement of her feet.

She practically floated to him, stopping as he met the three of them. Meera and Lyla pulled her into one last hug, and she held them tightly before whispering her thank-you's that could never fully express the depth of her gratitude for all they had done for her. They parted ways and joined the rest of the bridesmaids before Ronan took Sylvie's hands. That's when everything truly melted away.

"You're the most beautiful woman I've ever seen," he whispered in her ear as they stepped up to the officiant. She felt her cheeks flush as she kept her eyes on his, holding his hands as if letting go would cause her to fall. Her whole life prepared her for this all-consuming type of love. It's a type that not many can experience without losing all sense of reality.

They said their traditional vow, promised to love each other through everything that may come their way, and their words were sealed between looks of passionate devotedness, and promises that words could not articulate as meaningfully as their locked eyes.

"You may now kiss the bride," the officiant declared jubilantly, and Ronan pulled her to him so quickly, she lost her breath. His lips collided with hers, soft and eager, smiling into hers as he held her close to him. She laughed as he pulled away, and he kissed her once more, lips turned up so brightly that it sent new creases at the corners of his sparkling eyes.

Cheers erupted from the guest, their whistles, and claps resounding as the stringed instruments began again. They headed down the aisle, but Ronan stopped them halfway.

"What are you—" She barely got out her question before he swept her off her feet and kissed her again. His soft lips caressed hers as the cheers turned to whoops, and he partially brought his head back to look into her eyes, chuckling before tracing a finger down her flushed cheeks.

"I love you, Sylvia May Ashton."

Her brows tensed together as she searched his face with earnestness. "I love you, Ronan Ashton."

They kissed one last blissful time before lacing their fingers together and heading to the green house for their reception. Every moment of the evening was incredible, toasts and candlelit dinner with soft music carrying on in the background. It was the most unbelievable evening, Sylvie thought to herself just before Ronan stood up from the table, tapping his knife on the back of a pastel glass.

The room went silent, and Sylvie widened her eyes as she tilted her head as he grinned down at her.

"Thank you all for being here to celebrate our love. We are blessed to know each one of you and so thankful to call you our family. Today marks a significant day, not just because I've married my incredible wife."

Sylvie felt her cheeks grow a new shade of red as everyone awed in her direction.

"I don't think there is anything I could give Sylvie that could ever repay her with the type of love she exudes for everyone every single day. But, I want to try."

Sylvie looked toward Meera in question, who only shrugged.

"My gift for my Sylvia May is one that I've already given to her, but I've been waiting until tonight to share it as a promise to her and to you all... Ashton housing will no longer be doing business in Starwood. From now on, the only way anyone is visiting this town is through North Star Bed and Breakfast. We can have our business anywhere in the world, my dad saw to that with his incredible business model. But, there's only one North Star, and everyone deserves to experience it with the quaintness our town deserves to maintain."

Sylvie's jaw dropped, practically hitting the flower-covered table beneath her elbows. That must have been why he convinced her not to close North Star down, why he promised she would have guests soon enough, and within a week, she did. Tears spilled from her eyes. The room grew silent again when Ronan raised his glass.

"To my true love, and to North Star!" he cheered, and everyone cheered back in unison, beaming smiles and clinking glasses as Ronan sat down next to her.

"You didn't have to do that for me." She pressed her hand to his face, bringing him closer.

"Sylvia May, I would do just about anything for you. Not because I *have* to, but because I *want* to." He pressed his forehead to hers, catching a tear that fell from her eyes, before fervently eagerly kissing her.

She wasn't wrong when she thought his kiss was so true that it could end all curses in fairy tales. At that moment she knew, it could end all curses in the real world, too. And perhaps, love was always at the core of her North Star, his love—the devout, sacrificial, reckless type of love that is best felt rather than articulated.

Although many things would change in their world, as inevitably as the seasons, one thing would always remain constant in their love and lives: their slice of the world would be kept quaint and simple, with exciting visitors adding character to Starwood's already collegial sense of family.

As Sylvie looked across the familiar faces around her, she felt nothing but the love that no doubt donned the entirety of their town. With their support propelling her forward, nothing could stop her from conquering everything she wanted from life. That much was clear in the way they came to celebrate her and Ronan's love.

It was never more apparent that at the beating heart of

their world, North Star Bed and Breakfast promised to be a timeless landmark for perseverance, hope, and the tangible evidence of love prevailing.

That much would always be true for everyone brave enough to dream.

~

Tap Here To Continue To Book 2

Leave A Review

Like This Book?

Tap here to leave a review now!

Sneak Peek - Chapter 1

STARWOOD PROMISES

L ate at night, when everything was quiet and the world moved at a slower pace, Meera's mind always seemed to come alive in a way it hadn't during the day. She couldn't sleep—hadn't slept well for twenty years. Her fingertips traced over the edges of the tweezers on her desk, their cold metal alerting her of how quickly the steel she'd just torched would cool if she didn't set the stones in it.

Jewelry making was more than a hobby at this point. For Meera, it was therapy. One that she could not go without if she'd hoped to get some sleep during the night's long hours.

She peered through the magnifying glass, getting a better look at the steel she had mixed with the gold that she'd found in one of the thrift stores up the coast. Steel and gold were not a likely pair, but their combination created the most beautiful swirled effect. Unique, akin to the rings she would be gifting her best friend Sylvie and her husband Ronan. They had just gotten married half a year ago, but it was almost Christmas, and they were still wearing the old twisted bolts from North Star's initial build.

The ring she was working on was Sylvie's, and she did so with diligence, trying to push away the thoughts that haunted her. There were many, though the strongest, most prominent one, was a recent occurrence. Something she couldn't bring herself to ponder because she knew she had no way out of it. She sealed the final edges of the ring, placing the square-cut WELO opal. In the center, she dropped a hot pea-sized blob of metal and shaped it into a diamond before placing a small circular Moissanite gem in the very center.

"Please come home for Christmas, Mom." Chani, Meera's eldest child's voice, echoed in her head as she took a beat to admire her work. She shook her head, so the thought would fall out with her efforts, but it lingered like the anxious pit in her stomach. She brought the ring closer, observing all its qualities, attempting to further push the crisis away.

The band of the dainty ring was without flaw as it split in two on each side, connecting to each corner of the gemstone that was lined with tiny metal bulbs layered delicately. It was a sight to behold, truly incredible. But it didn't get rid of her frustrations and apprehensions.

It wasn't that she didn't want to go home for Christmas. On the contrary, she would have loved to see her children, to spend time with them in the place she raised them, but it was, perhaps, the thought of walking through the front door of her old home in Manhattan that scared her more than anything.

Meera had made peace with never going back to the house she'd left behind to help Sylvie start a new life. She could work in her marketing role, the one she'd had for twenty years, remotely while continuing to work for Sylvie on the side. She knew she belonged in Starwood, and she had tried to get her children on board with spending Christmas with her at North Star, but the suggestion didn't stick.

Now, she was done with both Sylvie and Ronan's rings, yet she didn't feel the least bit tired. Everything was rushing through her mind like an endless cycle of unwanted worries. She did not want to go back to that house, and that was the most prominent feeling. Perhaps, Chani was right to say it would be good for her to visit the home. Though, at that moment, Meera couldn't think of a worse place to go. She didn't want to think about why that was.

Instead, she set the rings in a secure spot, crossed the room to her bed, and crawled under the covers, attempting to take steady breaths.

Soon enough, even with the assaulting thoughts scraping over her mind, she was able to sleep—or pass out from exhaustion—but neither would work, considering she had such a busy day when the sun rose.

"Merry Christmas!" Sylvie peeped her head in the door, her golden brown waves curling around the edges of the door as she grinned sleepily. Meera knew by the heaviness of her eyelids and the stiffness of her lips that she hadn't slept long at all. But Sylvie was clearly well-rested, ready for Meera's last day at North Star for the holiday season.

"I brought you hot chocolate." She slipped inside, bare feet tapping across the hardwood before sitting on the edge of the bed. It barely dipped under her tiny frame as Meera propped herself up with pillows.

"I'm sorry I won't be here for *actual* Christmas." Meera sniffed, rubbing her eyes, still clouded with sleep.

"Shh." Sylvie shook her head, and extended the hot chocolate to her. "As far as everyone at North Star is concerned, today is Christmas."

"Syl, you really didn't have to do this." She took the hot chocolate, feeling her cheeks flush a little. All of this early celebration was for her benefit. The moment Sylvie knew Meera was visiting her children in the mainland, that was it. Ronan and her were talking a mile a minute, planning some grand day for them to celebrate the holidays together.

"I know. We want to. You do and have done so much for me and North Star..." She shook her head with a small sigh of affection. "You deserve to experience Christmas here, with your other family."

Meera felt her lips curl up as she buried her face in her mug, taking a sip of the thick and creamy, spicy hot chocolate. A speciality that Chef June always got just right.

"Thank you." She reached for Sylvie's hand, giving it a squeeze before placing the cup on her nightstand.

"Breakfast will be ready in half an hour. Come down ready to open gifts!" Sylvie clapped, standing and crossing to the door before Meera could comment on the plural that Sylvie had used. The door closed as she swung her legs over the side of the bed.

It had truly been so wonderful living with her best friend, and she was so thankful for the opportunity to be in such a wonderful, loving home. Especially during the holidays.

She climbed out of bed, crossing the cool floors with her bare feet and grabbing her thick ruby robe off the hook in the corner of her room. After braiding her curly black hair to the side, she headed to her work desk, where the rings were secured in a little, velvet emerald box.

It was small in her hand, but she knew the significance it held, and she was so thankful Ronan had let her take the rings unquestionably. Somehow, he'd convinced Sylvie to take hers off, and now, they were beautiful, new, and thankfully looked nothing like a piece that could hold furniture together.

She reached for the gold ribbon at the corner of her desk and wrapped it around the box before tying a bow on top. Her stomach fluttered with glee as she slid into a pair of slippers and headed out. Christmas music echoed through the halls, Sinatra's vocals bringing memories of deep joy to the wonderfully decorated B&B. The entire place was lit with fairy lights, Christmas garland, dancing stuffed elves and snowmen and Santa's. It looked like the North Pole rather than North Star, and maybe, that was the point.

Meera listened to the sweet chatter of cheerful guests and their children, already excitedly gathered in the dining room. She rounded the last set of stairs, walking down to the foyer as Sylvie and Ronan whispered to each other by the front door.

Seeing Sylvie happy was a magical thing, a sweet gift of its own. As long as she'd known her best friend, she'd never known her to be this loved or known by someone else apart from her. Ronan was a perfect match for her.

Sylvie turned around when she heard Meera's slippers connect with the foyer floor, a beaming smile on her face as Ronan turned in the same manner.

"Merry Christmas!" His warm voice chorused with Sylvie's soft and sweet one.

"Merry Christmas." Meera nodded softly, looking between them.

"Breakfast anyone?" June stepped around the corner, holding up silver trays on either side of her head.

"Let's go!" Ronan clapped, and Sylvie linked her arm with his as she chuckled.

Meera trailed behind everyone as they followed June into the dining room. The large fireplace was lit and roaring. The crackling audible even with the glee of the guests as June entered with starters. Meera found a seat next to a family from Germany that she'd spent a few hours with in the greenhouse yesterday.

She asked them many questions about their lives back home, and it sounded dreamy. Traveling was something she hadn't done much of. Being a single mother didn't really allow flexibility. Nor did her demanding life or college-aged children who still needed her close enough to them that if a crisis were to arise, she'd be able to drop everything to help.

As the courses came out and everyone's eyes lit up with delight, Meera felt the true sense of home. The gleam of the holiday season and what it truly meant to enjoy the company of the people she loved. Though it was not actually Christmas, it felt more like Christmas than it had in a very long time.

When breakfast was over and everyone had made their way to other activities, Ronan, Sylvie and Meera gathered around the tree in the front room to exchange gifts.

"You go first." Sylvie pointed to Meera's gifts sprawled out in front of her.

"This is insane, you both know that, right? I didn't need this many presents."

Ronan waved a hand dismissively. "Eh—*need, want.* Who's to say, sometimes, they're not one and the same?"

"Mhm." Meera smirked, blinking sarcastically at them both before opening the first gift. It was not a massive box, but inside, the gift was more meaningful than any she'd gotten before. A new blow torch, small and perfect for the work she did making jewelry. Not that the jewelry would go anywhere but on her or her friends, but it was a sweet and thoughtful gift nonetheless.

"You guys..." Meera breathed.

"You like it?" Sylvie raised her brows, pulling them together a bit.

"Yes, yes. This is...it's spectacular. A very, very generous gift."

"Oh, good." She sighed, grinning over at Ronan, who

beamed back at her, pressing his tongue to the inside of his cheek. They always used this unspoken language that only they could understand. Perhaps, they didn't realize it, but Meera did. And it should make her feel lonely, she thought. Any reasonable widow would feel that way after losing so much, but really, it just made her deeply joyed to know that type of love still existed in the world.

As she continued to open her gifts, there was an obvious theme. Most of the items were geared toward her hobby, though she never really spoke about it. Sylvie knew her best, had since they were little, but she mostly kept her jewelry-making to herself. It was easier that way, less disappointing.

She'd wanted to start her jewelry business so long ago, but that was a dream she never was able to achieve. Dreams were mere hobbies in her family. Jobs that paid for a secure lifestyle were practical careers. So, she followed what they told her and always respected their wishes for her.

Sylvie knew that, so why had she gone out of her way to give such an extravagant array of jewelry-making gifts?

"Well, I am completely honored to know you both. Thank you for the beautiful gifts. I'm afraid I only have one to give you both."

"Meera, you didn't have to get us anything. Your company is enough. This was just to honor you, and the things you love that maybe don't get as much attention as you'd like to give them."

"Well... Yes, but, I have so much to be thankful for, right?"

"Of course. We just wanted you to feel like your

dreams were just as important as Sylvie's. You've done so much to help her make hers a reality. It was only fair that we help return the favor."

"Oh..." Meera forced a smile that she knew didn't reach her eyes. She was not going to pursue anything like that. Hadn't planned to, and knew that it would not be respected by her family. After years of working on one career path, to change that now would only be foolish. Especially in her family's eyes. "Well, I really love the gifts very much."

"We love you very much." Sylvie said, reaching over the coffee table and giving Meera's hand a squeeze.

"Well, I hope you also love my gift." She reached into the pocket of her robe and pulled out the box, handing it to Sylvie, who retreated back to Ronan's side. Slowly, she pulled the bow open and gently lifted the lid of the velvet box.

There was a beat where the two of them stared intently at it. Eyes not fully readable as they grew rounder by the moment.

"So..." Meera swallowed the knot in her throat, hoping there was going to be some sort of reaction to her work.

Sylvie's hazel eyes panned up slowly from the box, tears brimming the edges as she sucked in her pink, quivering lip.

"These are the most beautiful pieces of jewelry I've ever seen, Meera." She whimpered, and Ronan nodded fervently.

"You've outdone yourself, Meera." He added as he pulled Sylvie's ring out of the box and slid it onto her ready finger. She did the same for him, and Meera watched with deep pride and immense relief. Her hard work was not only loved but represented love.

"It's made from the steel of your old rings."

"Ronan told me he took them to get cleaned." Sylvie's jaw dropped, corners of her mouth turning up as she longingly eyed him.

"I didn't know what Meera wanted them for, but I figured it had to be something related to her incredible jewelry that she wears." Ronan wrapped an around Sylvie's shoulders, and she rested her head on his, admiring the ring on her finger.

"You really need to start your own business, Meera." Sylvie's eyes practically glowed as she titled her hadn't back and forth.

"I don't know..." But she did know. She was not in any position to start that type of business. There was too much going on, and maybe the excuses would stop some day, but that day was not any time soon.

"Well, whatever you choose to do with your jewelry, we'd be happy to help in any way we can," Ronan offered, and Sylvie agreed.

"Thank you both." Meera did not plan to take them up on that offer, but she meant what she said. She was beyond grateful for the way she was able to live and the place she called home. Her job was a part of life, apart from honoring her family's legacy of hard work in fields that paid proper amounts. Curative jobs just didn't promise any of that. They were a gamble, and she couldn't take the loss if her life-long hobby crashed and burned.

Especially when it was something so vital for her to function.

***

After spending the day enjoying the company of gleeful guests and forever friends, Meera headed upstairs to pack. The ferry left at exactly 8 p.m., and she had to leave in fifteen minutes. She threw things into her duffle bag, knowing that she'd have some things at her house in Manhattan.

Traveling there to see her children was good. It would be a nice time, she told herself. But the more she tried to convince herself, the less sure she was that she could do this. That she could go back home.

It didn't feel like home anymore, and the idea of being back was not the only anxiety swirling in the pit of her apprehension. Maybe, she couldn't face the music yet, couldn't take her brain out of the gear it had been in while staying in Starwood.

Down the stairs and out the door with Sylvie by her side, Meera wanted to ignore the dread creeping up on her. After all, she should feel this way about spending time with her children. She loved them and reveled in the time she got to spend with them.

As Sylvie dropped her off at the ferry, she tried to shake away the nerves, push down what she knew was the thing truly causing them. The problem with stuffing her feelings was that they always found a way to come back in the worst forms. She knew it was coming, saw it like a small storm cloud on the horizon as she stepped off the ferry and into a cab.

But the truth of her anxiety didn't hit just then. Not until she stepped through that old faded green door, breathed in the all too familiar scent of lavender and cedar wood, and reached for the light switch so sure she'd burst into tears at the sight before her.

Bleary eyed, she could no longer ignore what had been eating away at her for the past few days. Perhaps even longer than that—much, much longer than that.

Sneak Peek - Chapter 2

SECRETS AT SILVER RANCH

With every light on in her home, she could see every face in every picture frame, smiling back at her. Sahil's kind smile, somehow, made the freezing house warmer.

"I'm home," she instinctively whispered to no one. It was shaky and rather pathetic as she stepped forward through the collage of family photos. In every one of them, Sahil was front and center, laughing, holding her hand, smiling at her as she played with the kids. The home was a shrine to someone who had passed nearly twenty years ago.

As she made her way through the hall and into the living room, her world became so much smaller. The things that mattered felt like nothing more than background noise.

She made her way to their bedroom, kissing her fingertips and pressing them to his cheek in a large mural of them before heading to their closet. It was full of clothes, smelt like him, too. Somehow, she had preserved his presence in this house like a time capsule. She couldn't be here, not because she didn't want to, but because she physically needed to move forward. She knew it the moment she left Manhattan for Starwood, but it was just now making itself fully known.

"Mom?" Chani called as the front door creaked open. Meera pressed her palms to her cheeks, wiping the tears and sniffing away the pain she felt before responding.

"In here, honey."

Chani's footsteps grew louder until they stopped at her doorway.

She paused, and must have been able to tell from Meera's frame how deeply distraught she truly was.

"How are you feeling?" she finally asked, gently, almost high-pitched.

Meera turned around, plastering on a grin she had mastered over the years of hiding her pain. "I'm all right, Chinnu."

For the first time, it seemed as though Chani wasn't buying this. Her eyes trailed the creases Meera knew framed her eyes and mouth from forcing her face to lie for her. Her daughter's brows tightened and lowered, as if she'd never noticed how human her mother was. She didn't like the way it felt to be analyzed like this, so she turned away and got to unpacking. Chani didn't say a word as she joined her, helping fold and put things away in the silence Meera had chosen.

By the late evening, they crashed in her and Sahil's bed, scrolling through the available channels on the tv. After the silence had become a ringing in the air and the tv was just on to bring some sort of noise to the room, Chani turned on her side, studying her mother.

Meera didn't want to talk, but Chani was even better than her at bringing out the truth in people, even better than she could.

"Mom, I know you would rather not be here."

"What? No, Chinnu. I love being here with you." She took her hand and brought it close to her chest, trying to meet her gaze with sincerity.

"Mom," Chani whispered. "You don't have to pretend anymore. I'm old enough to see how miserable this all makes you feel."

Meera wanted to disagree with her, but the truth had already engulfed everything in her being. Clearly, she was not okay, and maybe, she hadn't been since the loss of her husband. She'd stayed in the same job, left the house as it was because it was less painful than letting his memory die altogether.

There was no sugar-coating it. She was a mess, and she'd buried it, let her life stall because she couldn't move on, and convinced herself it was what she needed to do to stay afloat.

"You shouldn't have to worry about your mother this way, Chani."

"I know, but I want to. You've done so much for me and Nishan. We are forever grateful to you."

There it was again, that same phrasing that Sylvie had used. She was always doing so much for everyone else that she failed to see how her life stood completely still.

Everyone else was moving on with their lives, and perhaps, she wanted the same thing.

"Come here." She pulled her daughter close to her, snuggling Chani. Nothing could be done to reverse the years she'd spent, trying to keep things the same while helping others change. But perhaps, something could be done about it now.

As Chani drifted to sleep in her arms, a calm rushed over her like a cool river, carrying her down the stream of her life. She played back moments when she'd chosen others over herself, and she didn't regret one bit of it. She'd decided to push people to their fullest potential to stop herself from reaching hers. Because maybe reaching hers meant really letting go of Sahil and his memory, and ultimately breaking that promise she'd made long ago.

It had to be her time; she couldn't live this way for the rest of her life. Now was her moment to take back what she had too willingly given up—her own life.

Christmas was a blur of her children squabbling like they were in high school again, fighting over decorations and food and traditions. Her son came in a few days after Chani, and the continual back and forth between them started the moment he walked in the door.

Meera had decided to stay out of it, let them work it out instead of picking sides, and eventually, by the end of their time together, the two had somehow made it work between them. Perhaps, that's what she needed to do in every area of her life—stop working on things that will work out themselves and focus on the dreams that had laid dormant for too long.

Dreaming was selfish. *Was*, but she was beginning to realize how it was also selfish of her not to try. She'd spent far too much time on self-preservation, and that could have been why she was too afraid to try.

As she walked out the front doors of her home, hugging her children one last time before she headed back to Starwood, she knew everything would work out for the best. Whatever that meant, she was going to let go of the things she needed to and hold fast to the desires she'd neglected.

Click Here To Continue Reading

Also By Molly Summers

Castle Beach Sunsets Series

Second Chances At Castle Beach (Book 1)

Second Chances At Castle Beach (Book 2)

Second Chances At Castle Beach (Book 3)

The North Star B&B Series

Book 1 - Starwood Dreams

Book 2 - Starwood Promises (Coming Soon!)

Book 3

Book 4

Book 5

Book 6

Made in the USA
Coppell, TX
24 February 2023